Life Sliding

S.L. Mauldin

TouchPoint
Press

LIFE SLIDING by S.L. Mauldin
Published by TouchPoint Press
4737 Wildwood Lane
Jonesboro, Arkansas
www.touchpointpress.com

ISBN-10: 0692629726
ISBN-13: 978-0692629727

Editor: Tamara Trudeau
Cover Design: Colbie Myles, colbiemyles.com
Cover Photo: Joseph Wilson
Model Credits: Curt Roland and Talin Mattocks

Connect with the author online:
https://www.facebook.com/LifeSliding
Twitter: @SLMWRITES and @LifeSliding

First Edition

Dedicated to those who have ever felt alone at times or a bit of an outsider. And for YOU, for listening and following through with what I asked. Special thanks to Donna Ayers, Terri Roland and Curtis Roland.

A heart has many rhythms.
A beat when we're happy.
A beat when we're sad.
A beat when we're either stressed or mad.

Sometimes those beats can stop.

...in the grown up world

Those dreams where I'm trapped in a hallway at school were coming more frequently. This time, I didn't recognize anyone, but I sensed that I knew them. Their faces conveyed expressions of disappointment, with me I gathered. As I tried to escape, their faces changed and everyone began laughing. The laughing grew louder and louder and suddenly, I realized I was naked.

Just as my hands covered my ears to drown out the increasing laughter, the most annoying sound blared out, bringing me back to another unpleasant situation — called morning. It was likely that I had unconsciously pounded snooze more times than I should have. Late in the night when you are reluctant to go to sleep, you never remember the pain of dragging yourself out of a cozy bed, especially when you have to be somewhere on time.

When the light from the hallway hit me as the door swayed open, I tugged a pillow over my head.

"Gavin, get up!"

Groaning, I said nothing and within seconds, I was snoozing again when I heard the irritating click of my bedroom light. "Gavin."

"Dad, really?"

"Really nothing. Your alarm has sounded on and off for thirty minutes. Get up!"

"Oh my God. Do you have to come into my room every morning and do this?"

"Apparently I do if you can't haul yourself out of bed on your own."

"Like you ever give me a chance before you start nagging."

"Watch it."

"Watch what?"

"Gavin, get dressed. Now! You and I are going to have

a conversation this morning. This attitude has gone unchecked for too long and it's unacceptable."

#

What my dad rudely planted on me during that scathing lecture set the pace for a day of misery. Along with his other pleasantries about my attitude, Dad informed me that he was sending me away for the summer. I'm sure I looked stunned, but what could I say? Under those circumstances, I knew it was time to shut-up because one more word that was brazen might have hindered my liberties during my upcoming senior year.

Forget math and science or anything else for that matter because going away for the summer was the only thing owning my mind during my first four classes. From the first warning bell on, I counted down the seconds until lunch. By then I craved freedom from the teachers' "blah, blah, blah" which was all I heard basically; that and the mental looping of the early morning commandments from dear old Dad.

CLICK. Taylor latching her locker door sounded louder in the empty hall than it might have had it been buzzing with other students.

"Gavin, let's forget about lunch, I'm fat."

"Give me a break. Now, Chloe, she is the fat ass."

Most of our fellow parasites were planted in classrooms filling their minds with debris while others waited patiently in the lunch queue for their daily shovel of instant mashed potatoes painted with some powder and water mixture trying to pass itself off as gravy.

My high school was no different from others and nowhere was it more obvious than the cafeteria. Just as the oceans divided the continents of the world, labels segregated the tables. Due to changing demographics and employment possibilities for parents, kids were relocating from other cities. It seemed like hairstyles, fashions, and dialects were evolving with every school term. However, one thing that remained constant was that the cliques appeared blatantly evident whether it was clothing choice, lingo, race, or financial status.

Individually, I'm doubtful anyone would admit it as truth, but one thing everyone had in common was an unspoken desire to take another step up the social ladder. Ingrained within us on some level is a need to feel we're okay, and a change in one's status somehow solidified acceptance. Within the factions there were a few students who managed to cross the invisible boundaries. They experienced bits of other cultures and categories, but for the most part everyone clamped onto whatever held familiarity. My group — well, we never dabbled.

I knew we were all the same underneath despite the colors and titles people put on display. Most people never give it any consideration, but both popularity and unpopularity hold a price. Unfortunately, neither party can quite grasp this idea while struggling for its own place in the world. Each status has a sales tag.

For myself, I knew what I'd become, where I stood, and what I believed were my responsibilities in life. Even though I owned the title, what does "The Most Looked Up To" mean exactly? Whatever the criteria, I thought it was a ridiculous category for a yearbook heading, especially when the electorate was comprised of people who spend most of their waking hours gaming or updating their whereabouts on social media. Not to mention the fact that society's idea of beauty is typically an airbrushed and edited version of the real thing. What media pushes as reality is not reality at all.

As time went by, being "The Most Looked Up To" became extremely exhausting. While trying to be worthy of the spotlight, I could never just be *me* while I constantly constructed a persona.

Since I felt hopelessly trapped in a self-inflicted prison, I stuck with one color from the box of crayons. At that point, what could I do other than play along with the script I helped write? After all, the co-writers had expectations of who I should be. That was my reality.

The dream that held me trapped in a hall of worn lockers and laughing bystanders made sense to me. If I exposed the real me, would people laugh?

Approaching the cafeteria, Taylor reached for the door. "Don't forget to smile."

"What? I'm happy."

"And the dread on your face isn't a dead giveaway at all."

Avoiding the painted mash, we breezed through with our plastic food trays selecting our meal choices. The faces of the personnel clearly reflected their disdain for slopping out meals to teenagers. Maybe they hated their position in life or perhaps they simply detested their profession. Thinking about their plight, I pondered how anyone ended up with such a career as my dad's words rang out in my head, "Do you want to end up…" Briefly, I'd tuned him out and now he was back with a reminder of an impending summer of service imposed at my sentencing early this morning.

As the routine went, my friends Austin, Jayden, Chloe, and Grace were already in position at our designated table when Taylor and I arrived. Another long-standing tradition was that Taylor and I always intentionally appeared later as if we held some important secret in the societal underground that delayed us from getting there at the same time as the rest of the group. In reality, we were doing nothing special. It was just part of the show and kept the crowds guessing which made us seem even more interesting, unreachable, and elevated. That is what we thought, although the truth was that behind the flashing lights and vamped up exterior we were like every other Joe. However, with the flare and theatrics it was hard for anyone to see beyond the idea of what they thought we represented. We were the two standing on the top rung while others were trying to catch up.

"S'up guys?" Taking a seat, I lifted a limp slice of pizza, "This couldn't get any better. Cheap pizza in a room full of losers."

"Gavin," Taylor lightly nudged my side with the back of her hand, "speaking of loser."

Of course I glanced upward, but I veered away just as quick without a responding as I contemplated how many times over the past few years this topic came up.

Never one to filter herself, Taylor motioned her finger. "Austin, check that out. It's getting worse."

Revealing his disgust, Austin's words spilled with a southern drawl, which almost streamed as one jumbled sentence. "Where does he find that stuff?"

Showing us up, Jacob strolled through the cafeteria and I must say his appearance was a worthier show with his flair for dress and all. Even the confidence in his stride showed admirably considering his attention grabbing style. On the streets of London's West End in the 80's, he might have qualified as a candidate for a photo op with the clamoring tourist, but not here, not in average town. What Taylor said was true; Jacob's inventive choice of attire had gotten more outlandish since he showcased his fashions one early morning during our sophomore year. I respected his courage, but I loathed the endless dribble about him that had gone on ever since.

Taylor continued. "Gavin, do you think he bought that crap in a secondhand store or did he inherit it from his grandfather?"

My blond-haired sidekick Taylor was ruthless, blunt and though I would never say it aloud, I sometimes viewed her as the female version of myself. That applied to her outward guise only because whatever went on behind her green eyes remained reserved for those skilled in the art of mind reading. Since we'd put up with each other's shit for so long, her sordid statements had become as habitual as what body part gets washed first in the shower. Therefore, I often tended to ignore her harsh comments.

Usually I refrained and though I despised expressing anything on the sore subject, I did.

"His parents have the bling. I don't think his stuff is discount. Unique? Yes, as unique as whatever this sketchy pizza is made out of." I dropped the slice, "Chloe, you want this?"

In private, we boys regularly joshed about Chloe's extra buttery pounds. Not that she was morbidly fat, but no doubt, she could've used a few months at the gym with a personal trainer. As absurd as it sounded, even within our own clique there was an unspoken hierarchy. Chloe filled in the second position from the bottom since she lost points on an unforgiving body mass index scale.

"No, I'll pass, I'd rather not drop dead suddenly during language arts. I'd at least like to make it through the week," Chloe grew excited, "then summer break is on! Right, Grace?"

With a fist, Grace's right arm drummed the air

overhead, "I know, right? Whoop, whoop!"

Chloe probably meant what she said since school food is a silent killer, but that didn't stop her from picking at the stringy cheese and shoving it in her mouth. With a quick dart of our judging eyes, Austin, Jayden, and I couldn't withhold a snicker. Sadly, Chloe was kind of an airhead in these situations and reacted as though our actions were motivated by her waggish comments with regard to dropping dead or perhaps we'd found something entertaining about Grace's spontaneous, annoying chant.

Since Grace was quite aware of our snickers and judgment, she knew better than to keep eating and pushed the leftovers to the side. "Jayden, what are your plans for summer other than avoiding the oldies? Oh, aren't you doing some football camp thing?"

"Waiting for the acceptance letter and if I don't get in I'm down for anything to stay out of the house. All my parents can talk about is the economy."

Responding to Jayden I added, "I hear ya, the economy crashes and suddenly it's like it's our fault."

"I know, right? My parents stay glued to the news. Always some crisis brewing with the government or something. They wouldn't notice if I was there or not anyway. Might as well go away and enjoy the summer."

Considering Jayden's deep, burly voice, it was difficult to translate his elusive plea for some needed recognition from his parents. He succeeded at getting their attention on the football field, however that talent was the only thing that distracted his parents from their sedentary suburban lives and taking any real interest in his. Perhaps as a family, sports were all they had in common, which explained Jayden's intensity about football. With his true emotions hidden in the words, I completely understood feeling out of place at home.

After experiencing a childhood where my parents constantly traveled, I'd gotten used to the independence and now I detested any form of attention from them. My friends and adoring fans had come to meet whatever needs I had. My mind rested in that false conviction.

When my parents divorced, Mom moved to the west coast under the guise of being closer to her brothers and sisters, when clearly it was to get away from my dad. Following her departure, I became a singular child in a single parent household. Though my dad wasn't always present when I was younger, he was a strict disciplinarian from afar. Even so, I admit to a certain degree that I was spoiled. The problem was that Dad had noticed my complacency. Adding another issue for me, I had to include him on the list of people to please.

"I'd give anything for my dad to return to the days when he didn't notice if I were home or not. He has gone balls to the wall talking about the value of money and doing good deeds. Two years ago his motto was buy it now and worry about the details later."

It was true that my dad had become a newfound monetary conservative, but before the markets tumbled, he freely spent lots of money and it was no secret. When he allowed it, I didn't mind helping spend the money either and there were times that his guilt for leaving me alone so much played in my favor.

Austin's brow flicked up and down with every twang. "Your dad? The guy who flew somewhere just to have dinner?"

Austin's parents were fond of one particular city in Texas, which they named him after. *Very original,* I thought sarcastically. Austin was positioned at the bottom of the heap in our clan of overly indulged brats and if it weren't for football, I imagine he would've been sitting at a different table. The only reason he made the team in the first place was because he was as big as an ox. On the field, it made no sense seeing that he was as clumsy as Mr. Potato Head. Chloe found him attractive, but suggested that hugging him was like latching onto a California redwood tree. Taylor had a different opinion about him altogether. Something more along the lines of a big turd, and she despised when Austin got overly excited which caused his Texas twang to resemble a foreign language. Personally, I would have to agree that on occasion his sentences needed translation. Austin was never invited in, but somehow he was always, just there. He balanced out the group in some weird way. I can't explain it really.

"That's the one. I used to wonder if he would ever come home again. Now, I wonder if he'll ever leave. The sudden interest in my life is so wack."

Feeling left out, Taylor threw in an empathy card from left field. "Guys, my mother used a coupon the other day. I mean, what is a coupon? So, uh, embarrassing."

All the negativity prompted buttery Chloe to remind us that it was almost summer.

"We need the have best summer ever. This is it. Next year we're seniors and if there is any truth to what the oldies say, we'll be scattered to the corners of the planet and shortly after that we'll be handcuffed to a corporation."

Chloe meant well, though her delivery only added to the gloomy conversation.

So much for shedding some positive vibes; why not add to the gloom? They had no idea of the horrible plans my dad had for my vacation this time.

"It's already over for me. My dad feels that I need to

do something worthwhile this summer." My voice turned sarcastic. "He has had a revelation. He wants me to reach out to humanity — a summer of torture basically. Why can't he do it himself if he wants to give something back? I haven't taken anything out, so why should I give something back? And that is how my morning started boys and girls, a speech from the king. Get this, he is forcing me to serve at a special needs camp this summer, whatever the hell that is."

Just as I was solidifying a somber mood, a plastic food tray crashed to the floor somewhere in the cafeteria causing an echo, and for a brief moment, the segregated parties broke into a chatty buzz as one.

"Doh, the pizza is already taking a toll." I spouted, getting a laugh.

Within seconds fists were flying. It turned out that one of the goons tripped a lesser goon and then a completely different goon threw a punch for revenge. It doesn't matter where anyone stands in the social order, there is always someone trying to get ahead by any means necessary. Apparently, a student walked too close to one of the protected boxes of familiarity.

Catching him out of the corner of my eye, Jacob jolted from a round stool and skimmed across the vast room to rescue the victim of an ultimate embarrassing situation. His blinding white shirt, dark red and black plaid pants, and a leather crisscrossed suspender contraption that hung down below his slim waistline could've been pulled from a Lady Gaga video. The whole time I expected him to trip over the flapping strands and end up sprawling across the floor himself.

The whole duration of the commotion, I kept my hand tightly clamped down on Austin's hairy arm trying to

15

restrain him from getting in on the action. He thought it would be fun, but I cannot imagine how suspension from the last few weeks of school would be worth it. For a moment, I was sure I heard Austin clicking his teeth together like a leashed dog about to lurch toward a floppy-eared bunny scampering across a lawn.

Due to the incident, rumors floated for days about bones getting broken, bloody noses, suspensions and who knows what else. Along with that, I was sure that Austin would make good on his word and take a slug at one of the kids involved in the fight because he believed they got away with a sucker-punch just as the fight was breaking up.

In the grown-up world, this behavior is referred to as war.

...for two years I waited.

"What a freak!"

Though it didn't come from my mouth, that blunt statement was the signal of change. For two years when Jacob wheeled onto the school grounds, the way I felt about it is difficult to express. Although the car stood out like a jellybean in a bag of marshmallows that's not what pricked my emotions because I had to admit the car was chill.

Since Jacob was financially privileged to the point where he could've had any make and model of car he wanted, I wondered why that one. After much contemplation in that regard, I concluded that the car was just like him – different. Considering the appearance, someone with a love for oldies went to great lengths to restore Jacob's silver 1967 Volkswagen Karmann Ghia to mint condition.

Even before peering up and catching a glimpse of the circular headlights, I always knew when Jacob arrived on campus. The rear-mounted engine held an original hum, distinctive of the Volkswagen brand. However, more demanding of my attention was the music blaring from inside the cabin, and the demanding glow of the pearly-white interior. Whatever played on that sound system was never comparable to any of the tunes my classmates had downloaded on their mp3 players. Not even close.

Since our last conversation, which took place the last day of school after surviving our freshman year, among other changes, we had both grown at least a foot taller. During that summer, we hadn't spoken because Jacob went off to experience something new and against my will, my dad dragged me all over the country while he attempted to regain the momentum in his sluggish business ventures. I never fully understood the details, but the media filled their airtime with tidbits about the historic glitches in the world economy. Because of certain situations, a short summer of separation created a divide between two life-long friends.

During the break from classes and teachers, I visited a majority of the prominent cities in the United States. Near the end of our travels, we had a 48-hour stint in London where I toured the city by looking out the windows of the 8th floor. It sounds exciting, yet to the contrary, most of my vacation revolved around massive airports, boarding airplanes, and viewing mindless television shows in the confines of overly priced hotel rooms. There weren't any holiday type activities during the jaunts except for the fact that I didn't have to do homework and most days I slept into the afternoon. The only way I refrained from gaining twenty pounds and kept fit was because I developed an insane obsession for doing push-ups, mainly due to excessive boredom. Along with that, at every opportunity, I insisted on carrying our bulky luggage through numerous lobbies, down long breezeways, and up stairwells.

For the first time in the history of summers, I was anxious to get back to school and to a bit of familiarity like hanging out with Jacob and the others. That year in particular, I anticipated the return to school since it was our opportunity as sophomores to harass the incoming freshman class. Even hanging out in the segregated cafeteria sounded appealing when compared to stifling hotel rooms and the trappings of sensationalized talk shows and readily available cable reruns from the 20th century.

On the first day of tenth grade, after returning from

months of touring, there I stood in the middle of the parking lot waiting. One by one my friends appeared, stood alongside, and while waiting we plotted our initiation for the incoming squad of pubescent boys and girls. My fellow classmates were taunted the prior year and it was our self-appointed right as tenth-graders to continue the tradition with the incoming class, whom we referred to as freshies. Just as we had, the freshies bravely put up a front by appearing unbothered by the surge into a new world, but we knew better. Back then, we thought we knew it all too. Adjusting to having more responsibility and acclimating to a life around older classmates, who too had lost their innocence not so long ago, takes time.

As that early morning of our tenth year proceeded, the booming serenade of music grabbed my attention straight away. I jested that Cirque du Soleil must be nearby, yet it was no circus, not as defined anyway. When that rare car made its first appearance, we were in awe. At first, we speculated the possibility of it being a transfer student and envied the fact that they were the owner of such fly wheels. Compared to the other two and four door sedans it was comparatively like parking a Bentley in a Toyota sales lot. It just didn't fit.

There was no way of knowing if I had spoken first if things might have gone differently, though in that moment, my mouth wouldn't move. I remained shocked the minute he rose out of the driver's side of that flashy car. Unrestrained, Austin blurted out "What a freak" with a thick Texan accent before I could grunt, clear my throat and make any sort of statement. Austin had no clue who it was I'm sure, until the person artfully removed a pair of silver-rimmed glasses followed with a cleverly flicked triangular wedge of brown hair away from his eyes. Jacob!

I could've said something, but I didn't and Austin set the tone for what followed. Time passed and although I never engaged in any of the taunting and catcalls, I did something much worse; I kept quiet while I stood right in the middle of what seemed like harmless teasing.

Realizing how we had developed the habit of hanging out in the school parking lot every morning before homeroom didn't hit me until later.

Ritualistically, since day one of my sophomore year I waited for something to change. I waited for signs. For almost two years, I waited for the old Jacob.

Now that my junior year was ending, my friendship with Jacob had become something obscure and in the past. The distance between he and I had grown so wide that I didn't know him any longer, not personally, and there were no indications that there would ever be a reunion between old friends. Every day, though, the reminder remained constant. That car.

#

Once I got through the hazy day and after a grueling football tryout for the following season, I went straight home. Settling in front of my computer to do my homework, I arranged the desk accordingly. Pretending to do my homework was more of an accurate description, because underneath my fake set-up I chatted with Taylor. It was taking her forever to respond in the chat-box and that was annoying enough even though I really had nothing else to do. There were my assignments, but…

We never discussed anything crucially important and our sessions often consisted of sending each other links to videos, music downloads or making fun of peoples' Facebook profiles mostly. Girls with duck lips. Boys with a snapbacks positioned oddly. Never leaving out the famous bathroom mirror pout where a prominent ball of light steals the spotlight from the object of the photo.

When I questioned Taylor about the lag in her response time, Taylor revealed that she had painted her fingernails and was pecking at the keyboard with a pencil. Knowing Taylor, I vividly visualized a towel tightly curling around her head, mud-mask on her face, and a left to right frantic search for the correct letter to peck. Totally explains why she misspelled the already shortened messenger abbreviations.

Thankfully, I had my cover when Dad knocked on my bedroom door because with one click of a button, the chat-box disappeared behind a window. Dad did not allow social networks — they are dangerous and a time wasting distraction, he said. Of course, I laughed when he pointed it out years ago.

"Gavin?"

He had a rule forbidding locked doors as well. Once I noticed the first signs of body hair I tried securing my room and just as quickly my dad informed me that I didn't have anything that he hadn't seen before and a locked door suggested I was hiding something. Then as the typical parent will do, he went on to suggest that when I bought my own house I could lock the doors that I had paid for with my own money. He eased up somewhat after my body's transformation resembled more that of a young man and granted a short pause before entering, but still no locks. Surely, he knew what teenage boys do, but I suspected his rule was more about control versus one of suspicion.

"Gavin, here is your itinerary. We are leaving at eight am that Sunday. Might be wise of you to take a break from the computer and spend some quality time with your father."

Perhaps he was more aware than I thought because he did say computer not homework.

Trying to hold back a laugh in response to his comment about quality time, I tugged the folder free from his grasp. Like I cared, I pretended to look inside at the material as he was leaving the room, but as soon as he was gone, I placed the folder to one side of the desk and moved to the bed. If we were to spend an evening together what could we possibly talk about — the news? The dangers of online predators? Supply side economics? No thanks!

Dread mounted in my stomach as I pondered the words "Lift Me Up" marked in bold black lettering on the cover of the manila folder; more so, of what that entailed exactly. My thoughts lingered and I wondered what motivated this sudden need for Dad to exercise his control and spoil my summer break? A second summer break ruined. In addition, why after years of spending quality time elsewhere without me was he so hell bent on me being included? I wanted to throw it out there that sending me away during the school break would separate the two of us, but he'd never fall for that plea because he was quick to catch on to psychological mind games.

#

My last week as a junior hurried by until the very last day of classes. It was 3:10 in the afternoon on what felt like one of the longest Fridays I could remember.

Each time I glanced at the large black numbers on the clock mounted on the block wall I was tempted to question the teacher as to whether or not the batteries were still working. I should have gone through with the inquiry because that would've conjured a good chuckle from the other students since I'm sure that time had stopped for them as well. Speaking out in such a silly manner was beyond the chill factor though, because my self-induced protocol required that I maintain a nothing-bothers-me attitude in every situation. The humorous role remained reserved for the person voted "Best Sense of Humor", otherwise known as the class clown.

I tapped the shoulder of the kid seated in front of me. "Do you have a watch?"

Finally, the bell chimed, time restarted, and like racehorses bolting from a gate, students hoofed out of the classrooms yelping and clamoring. The hall was mayhem and madness as discarded notebook paper floated through the air and onto the floor like giant pieces of confetti. Locker doors slammed loudly and several unconcerned students couldn't be bothered to shut them at all. Cracking me up, every fifteen feet sat a strategically placed trashcan, which remained completely empty throughout the afternoon parade. Even though I was a hard-ass, I held sympathy for the custodial staff required to clean up the remnants of tests, journals, and unfinished book reports. Not forgetting the randomly strewn candy wrappers and gym clothing that reeked a memorable stench.

Taylor caught up with me near the end of math hall and we exited through the nearest metal doors.

"Do you believe this shit? These kids must live in a trailer park," I said with disgust.

Taylor discarded an old notebook. "Animals."

We dodged in and out of the mismatched brick buildings making our way to the parking lot. It was a longer escape route, but better than being in the zoo trapped with the other animals.

"Taylor, look at her. She is in love with it."

From across the schoolyard I noticed Chloe leaning

against her car artfully ripping a wrapper off a candy bar.

"I gave her some diet tips, and I never mentioned chocolate."

Nearby, with her head cocked backward, Grace was letting the sun get a head start on a summer tan as she ran a tube of Carmex across her lips.

Next to Grace, Jayden and Austin were caught up in some football player ritual that from a distance looked like two orangutans in a standoff and all I could hear was a ridiculous drawn out, "Boyiz" as Taylor and I approached the scene. Seemed the zoo spilled over into the parking area.

Jayden, Austin, and I keened in on Chloe when she began discussing her exhausting plans for a diet over the summer.

"Do you guys know if watermelon is fattening?"

What made it even more hilarious was that every time there was a seasonal break from school Chloe had a treasure map to physical fitness and wanted all of us to be a part of it, as if we needed to. I started to throw out a pun, when I heard the familiar sound of the Volkswagen.

In his car, Jacob eased around a trail of lingering teenagers as music thrummed from inside the silver car and oddly, he turned, looking in our direction. A first in a long time, it was so unnerving when our eyes made contact as he vaguely nodded. I did the same and then he turned away. For a minute, I felt a chill. What the hell was that all about?

After a while, the vehicle that had at first gained admiration altered into something of utter disdain. It didn't look any different than it had two years ago and it was still a dope car, though I would never express my thoughts around the group. It was excessively late in the trip for me to redirect the train of contempt.

I surmised that Taylor noticed the exchange of nods and of course, as usual, she needed to comment.

"How pathetic is that? It's obvious that his parents are saving their money and not wasting it on him." Taylor flipped her long blond hair behind her shoulders.

Apparently, she had no idea the Karmann Ghia was a rare and valuable car.

The others volunteered remarks but, true to form, I remained a silent observer. The conversation in my head chattered louder than the voices of my friends; maybe I blocked them out on purpose and that spoke volumes.

…succumbed to endure for the summer.

With vengeance, the clock on the wall sped forward over the weekend. When the alarm clock rang out at eight am on Sunday morning, I wanted to stuff it between the mattress and box spring after fumbling around for the snooze button. Once I found the hidden control and started sinking back into the depths of slumber, the annoying buzzer warned once again. That time I jerked the cord out of the wall. Not too long afterward, my cell phone began to beat out a familiar ring-tone. Though I wanted to, I didn't dare hurl my lifeline out of the window and onto the lawn. I answered since it was Dad calling from downstairs and I would've regretted not doing so because that would've give him a reason to stop footing the bill for something he declared I had no need for anyway. Clearly, it only served as a means for monitoring me and keeping me under his formidable guidance.

Dad was habitually impatient and I wasn't a morning person. While I slept off the lingering effects of a party the night before, Dad was off gassing up the car for the ride over to where I would commit my service. I hadn't even showered, packed a bag, or eaten breakfast, but he was ready to leave. Before the collapse, along with other statements, "time is money" was one of my dad's favorite mottos. To be honest, I never understood any of the meanings to most of his sayings.

Dad bellowed through the phone, "What about eight am did you not understand? The buses have a schedule!"

I moved quickly while wondering why he couldn't drop me off at the camp; why a bus? "Lift Me Up" was less than an hour drive from our house according to what little I remembered him telling me about the place. Buses?

26

In a haze, I took a one-minute shower, grabbed some clothing and packed it away. Leaving the room, I heaved a bag on my shoulder and grabbed my cell phone from atop my desk.

I grew even more furious when Dad's car made a right turn into the vast parking lot of a big-box retailer where I noticed a row of worn-out yellow buses. How much humiliation did I have to go through to suit whatever purpose my dad had for sending me away for the summer?

During the ride over Dad lectured, but I only grasped one important detail.

"You need to understand that you're not the center of the universe. The reason I'm suspending your cell service is that I don't want you getting distracted. Texting and talking on the phone is not what you're there for."

To which I replied, "What? Are you kidding me?"

My vacation prison sentence gained another level of resentment straightaway. Whatever happened with the economy, his business, his life was rapidly encroaching on mine. I had one question on my mind, but I never said it out-loud. What did I do?

Slamming the car door, not bothering to say goodbye, I headed directly to someone who appeared to be in charge to inquire as to which one of the decrepit monsters I should ride in.

"Gavin Bailey."

Some geeky dude wearing a tacky visor, wielding a wooden clipboard motioned toward one of the buses half of the way down the row.

"2681 near the end."

I sneered as I watched my dad leave the lot in his luxury air-conditioned car.

After finding the correct bus, anxiously, I composed a

short text message informing Taylor about Dad's unreasonable decision to halt my cell services. I continued with whatever last conversations I could get in while waiting for the buses' departure. With difficulty, I tried ignoring all the people piling onto the bus with their backpacks and water bottles. In my head, I was the only one suffering. All I kept thinking about was why were these people so obnoxious, and how dare someone bump me with a sleeping bag. Along with those complaints, I would include that it was at least five degrees hotter inside our grand transportation to "Camp Do Good". In addition, what was with the way-too-skinny blond-haired kid who kept peeking over the rear of his seat and looking at me? And what was with the creepy dark water swimmer chick who kept peering over at the frail kid, and then glancing in my direction? Didn't their parents teach them that staring is rude?

There was no retreat in irritation by the time we arrived at Camp Lift Me Up. Even the signage with its happy welcoming struck me the wrong way. Lifted wasn't how I might have describe my feelings in that moment. The anxiety level crept up a notch when I stepped down off the large bus and staffers ushered us like a herd of cattle toward a rectangular chocolate-brown building that didn't look in much better condition than the vehicle that brought us there. Amongst the beauty of the surrounding greenery sat several buildings in need of a facelift. On the other hand, maybe a bulldozer was a better option.

The final sting of last night's beer pong seared through my skull and my brow wrinkled with both pain and tension as I entered the quickly crowding meeting area. Since looking around the tattered room made my turmoil worse, I should've closed my eyes. Varieties of backpacks covered the planked floor by the resting steel folding chairs that appeared as weathered as the exterior walls of the building. I pondered my comfort zone, the fact that I was suddenly and unwillingly forced to dabble.

Choosing a spot in the second row near the middle of the room, I flipped my phone open; thumbed the keyboard, responding to Taylor's last message. It was over, my last lifeline to the real world. There was no reply and my summer camp sentence grew gloomier.

Sarah, who was in her mid-thirties with curly brown hair and highlights that were an obvious do it yourself bottle job, stepped onto a platform. Her tanned face was as serious as her stiffly starched navy blue pantsuit, though the circular peace earrings threw me off track. Clearly, Sarah was comfortable in front of a large gathering, instantly coming across as very assertive. In my mood, even if it were my favorite band, I still would've found something in that situation that ticked me off.

"Thank you all for being here and volunteering your services for the summer. First, I will give you a brief introduction of the camp and cover a little of my history. It is most important to me that you remember, this summer isn't about me and it isn't about you. Keep that in the forefront of your mind."

My metal chair seemed smaller and harder every passing second. I attempted to follow the lecture, but seething through my veins was a need to tackle something on the football field. If it hadn't been for the physicality of football, I would've exploded a long time ago. Though I disliked the game, another area where I'd locked myself behind bars, I loved it as an outlet for pent up aggression.

"I founded Lift Me Up around eight years ago. I've dedicated my resources as well as my soul to the camp's success. Since I am just covering the basics, your assigned counselor that you will assist will cover the rules and go over the activities. I remind you once again that this process isn't about you. However, I will suggest that if you open yourself up to the possibilities and pay attention, you might learn something fundamental."

Since my hearing was in and out of consciousness, I stretched, raising my hand because like a clueless brat, I had questions.

"Yes?" Sarah inched out from behind a podium.

Sounding annoyed I questioned, "What kind of camp is this again?"

Of course, detailed information about the camp was available in the folder I failed to read and that folder rested where I wanted to be, at home.

In one motion, Sarah swooped down to a squatting position, catching me at eye level as she might do to address a small child.

"Part of life is about being prepared for tomorrow. The only time anyone should ever show up uninformed is at birth and the process should end around first grade."

Becoming clearer to me, Sarah was no stranger to dealing with unruly teenagers who purposely distanced themselves from the cruel realities of the world. When she spoke, it was as though she had been briefed about me in particular.

She stood up, turned away from me, which irritated me even more, so I started to raise my hand again when someone intentionally kicked my chair from behind. I lowered my arm as I turned around looking with a riled glare that would sear through skin.

"Sorry, too much coffee," the odd girl from the bus smirked.

I pivoted back around, fidgeting, while listening to what I figured was Sarah's way of answering my question for the whole room and slamming me at the same time. Need I suggest that I felt singled out in a room full of underdogs?

"As the material explained, the children will range in age from six to twelve years old. These children are from different backgrounds and have varying issues to manage. As trainees, your knowledge of those issues will be limited. Our goal is to treat the children as normal as possible under the circumstances life has dealt them. This is a brief moment in time where these children will be removed from their own environment and hopefully where they don't have to be anything but children."

Sarah eased closer to where I was seated, "I could compare this to, say, one of you who perhaps never had a laptop, a cell phone or the latest CD that dropped on Tuesday and for one single summer you did."

Her comments were clearly directed at me and because of that, I wanted to shoot a five-letter word that started with a *B* and leave right then. Holding my tongue, I waited it out and as the meeting concluded; I hastily grabbed my bag, planning to head straight out the door to find a phone.

"First time?" asked the strange, chair-kicking girl as she shifted her backpack higher on her right shoulder.

"And last I hope." I shoved my phone in the side pocket of my gear.

"Ah. I sense that your parents made you come against your will?"

"My father. He found his way back to the light after years of sucking the lifeblood out of capitalism like a deprived vampire." I shot back.

With a hint of understanding she continued, "The

economy?"

"Yeah, something like that. Who knows really, who cares? Suddenly I'm supposed to take an interest in his goings on. Amazing how a jolt to a hedge fund can change a man."

If I could've step outside myself at that moment, I would have stomped on my own foot. *Why did I keep engaging in conversation with this strange girl*, I asked myself?

Her hair was jet black, straight as a needle, her bangs cropped just above her eyes, and the side length ended near the top of her shoulders. Her eyes were almond-shaped, golden-brown. Each one of her painted fingernails was a different color and her shirtsleeves fell along the length of her knuckles. Her clothes were plain, black and accented by a white belt with an attached Hello Kitty pendant positioned near the buckle. Strange combination.

When her eyes shifted upward to the left, her facial expression altered and I couldn't begin to imagine what she was pondering inside her dark world where an animated pendant seems to be the only hope.

"Yes, those hedge funds," She turned serious, "well, just be thankful that your father was jolted in the right direction."

"I would be happier if the direction continued down the hall and away from my room."

"Right, poor you."

"Grief already? We haven't even introduced ourselves. I'm Gavin."

"Marissa. No grief, just an observation."

Where was that stomp? Again, I wondered why I was talking with this scary girl. I didn't know what else to say and truthfully, I didn't care to say anything, but I proceeded, rather unpleasantly. Angered by the entire day, I couldn't help myself.

"You rudely bumped my chair and now you're observing?"

"Does this charm come naturally for you?"

My ability to go on the defensive was much stronger than my ability to charm and it was time to end that conversation. I didn't mind ripping her apart in process. She was nothing to me. She wasn't a student from my school and she had no idea who she was dealing with.

"Ah, I know your kind. I had one in third period, third row five seats back. All black, bangs covering the eyes and all the right answers."

My body language alone expressed my outlook about her kind. Much to my surprise Marissa held strong with her stance and wasn't shaken by my jab.

"Pegged me. I know you too. Right shoes, haircut and an attitude that your friends mirror or vice versa."

"Sums it," I announced proudly.

As I shifted my travel bag to my other shoulder I heard a door spring shut and someone entered, grabbing my attention. Instantly my level of frustration reached a heart thumping high. There was no way in hell I was staying at this camp. I was already apprehensive, but when I watched him walking toward Sarah, any form of hesitation fled from my body. Suddenly, my naturally regulated breathing was interrupted.

Aware of the distraction, my obvious lack of interest in the camp or our chat, Marissa continued her offensive mode as she rolled her mood shifting eyes.

"If you'd rather send me a text message?"

"What? Never mind! Leave it! I got to figure a way out this!" I turned, leaving Marissa standing alone.

I knew I was close to home, but what was Jacob doing there? Had I died and gone to hell?

#

After storming off from the uncomfortable conversation with Marissa, I discovered an old tattered rotary payphone next to the lunch quarters. I retrieved a number from my cell phone because I didn't have it memorized and most likely, I had never actually dialed it other than pushing one button.

"Dad this place is ridiculous. If you could see this place — the freaks. I don't know anything about kids. Not to mention these other sheisty people."

I pleaded my case, used my persuasive talents, and made all sorts promises, but nothing changed his stance. Dad used three words during the entire call. Hello. No. Goodbye. Unless I wanted to run away, I had no alternative. There was always an option to call Mom, but since she jumped into a relationship with a younger man, her time for me was limited; at least that is how I viewed the situation. Besides, Dad would have warned her that I might call whining about being in a dire situation, so approaching her was pointless. Their relationship had fallen apart, but when it came to me, they remained united. Dad wrote the alimony checks, so what was mom going to do, go against his wishes? If one of Dad's early life lessons hadn't freaked me out about serial killers and male on male rape, I would've pitched a thumb and hitchhiked right out of there.

#

My assigned sleeping quarters, Cabin 7, sat in a row of other cabins placed in a series of four, perpendicular to another collection of four, 16 total that formed a perfect square. With room enough for bunks and a small pathway for mobility, the cabin only housed ten children and one CIT. I was a CIT, which is short for Counselor in Training, and my sole responsibility was to make sure the right kids were in the correct cabin at bedtime.

In the center of the box formation was a smaller cubed building that served as the communal bathroom. The facility was worn, but clean, yet I still didn't want to touch anything. The avocado green sinks probably appeared just as they did in the Sixties during their installation. The showers had no heads at all and streamed a solid flow of water.

The older counselors bunked together in their own area slightly further in the woods, which was more private with its own facilities. The only time the experienced counselors spent in our smaller quarters was once a week for a couple of hours in order to relieve one of us so we could have a night out. A night out didn't amount to much and a strict curfew still applied. As long as we were present for bed check and band-aid maintenance, we could stay up as long as we wished. For the young campers however, lights out was strictly enforced by nine pm. Lights, meaning battery powered lamps and flashlights, since the smaller cabins had no electricity.

The second time that I noticed Caleb was outside of Cabin 7 where I paused holding my travel bag while checking my cell phone hoping that Dad had come to his senses, caved, and restored the services. That was the least he could've done to ease the pain I was about to endure for the summer. No luck.

With a small crowd of other kids, Caleb drifted right by and I couldn't help but notice him, his appearance, and his inquisitive stare. He appeared frail, innocent and despite whatever was wrong with him, in some ways he looked angelic. As I observed him, he watched me intensely and I tucked away the cell phone for the last time. Caleb cracked a smile, his tiny hand thrust into the air waving, and I smiled and waved back as my brow unintentionally rose in acknowledgement. During the exchange, it seemed the other campers disappeared into the surroundings and Caleb and I were the only ones present. Then it hit me that he was the kid that kept peeking over the rear of the seat on the bus.

The young campers staying in Cabin 7 were overly excited and I could see them ambitiously pairing off and forming new friendships. In that small room, I witnessed the same territorial behaviors of people double their age. Just like the dining area at school, the like attracting like was fully manifesting right in front of me. Even in a spastic group of ten little boys, I could pick out the natural-born leaders and detect the quiet reserved types that might choose a table farthest from the cafeteria door back at school.

Once I made it inside and claimed a bed, I didn't bother unpacking. Placing stuff inside the small two-drawer chest would've signaled some kind of permanence. I still had hopes for a miracle, that Dad might call and I would be out of there and on my way back home where I could enjoy the summer break.

…a turbulent storm was brewing.

Through the first few days at camp, I kept to myself, only speaking when it was necessary. So many things can run through the mind when there aren't any gadgets around for distractions and using up hours of the day. I needed that silent process to help me settle into the fact that I was now part of "Lift Me Up" against my wishes.

The camp's limited links to the outside world were the antiquated rotary phone and a late model computer that we could use once a week for checking email. In front of me was the only form of visual stimulation, and that consisted of kids shooting each other with water guns or watching them play a friendly game of dodge ball, which they did with a beach ball for safety reasons.

For my other assigned duty, I shadowed an experienced counselor who was just a few years older than I was. There were no expectations for me to do much other than observe or assist when setting up for some activity and cleaning up afterward. I determined that eventually trainees graduated to a higher status during the summer or upon a second stay. I hadn't inquired since it wasn't important to me anyway. My list of short-term goals hardly included a return visit. My only aim was to keep my teeth unclenched until my parole at the end of the summer session.

In between the finer sport of archery and a carnival-style beanbag toss, I noticed Jacob patrolling the grounds of the camp. Seeing him in a toned down version of himself seemed odd since I hadn't seen him any other way in years. When I say toned down I mean he was wearing shorts and a tank top that almost resembled what I viewed as normal. What an odd twist that we ended up at the same camp, as if destiny stepped in and dealt a card from the deck of life. Or fate said, "Now take that. Let me make your summer more like hell."

Taking showers in the afternoon was the most uncomfortable situation that I could've ever imagined. Not only did I have the pleasure of lukewarm water pounding on my skin, I had to share the horrible moment with boys no older than ten. The only positive thing I could say was at least I had a showerhead all to myself while the younger boys had to share. Bathing with others at school was no big deal, but standing there bare-butt naked with little kids made me feel self-conscious. I chose the faucet closest to the wall and did my best to keep the front part of my body shielded from the others. I recalled my dad saying that I didn't have anything that he hadn't seen before but that provided no ease to the awkward circumstance.

#

Just after sundown, we were sitting around a campfire and the campers, guided by an older kid wearing a straw hat, sang corny songs back to back. Not that I wanted to join in, but I had never heard any of these songs before. The whole notion seemed silly, but I wasn't nine either.

"I wish I was a little yellow duck…"

Finally, the sing-a-long ended and Sarah, typical enthusiast, commanded everyone's attention. Her arms flapped out at her sides creating a whirlwind of excitement as the young campers gathered around her like ducklings would their mother. Sarah's eyes were wide open and she genuinely exuded a thrill. Right then, I wanted to vomit.

"Okay campers find a roasting buddy, then we'll pass out the marshmallows!"

I was standoffish, however I managed to stay present and pay attention to the activity going on around me.

Campers scurried about pairing up with their mates when my attention diverted to Marissa, who was off to the right side of the fire stooping over. With Caleb close at her side, I noticed him lift to his toes, cover his mouth, and whisper into her ear. Marissa rose and headed in my direction. I had seen her around involved in the daily activities, but I hadn't spoken with her since I blew her off at the meeting.

Marissa eased her way over.

"Oh charming one, if you're not too caught up brooding I have a request."

Marissa twisted a long strand of straw and since she sounded sincere, I responded with as much interest as I could muster.

"And what might that be?"

"Seems we have a little guy over here who finds you just as enchanting as the crowd that sits in the first four desks of third period." Marissa's head motioned toward Caleb.

Head twisting, I blurted out, "Oh, this is lame."

"Come on, there has got to be a heart underneath that arrogant exterior."

I inhaled a deep breath while motioning for Caleb to come over. Marissa was elated with my willingness to cooperate and help the kid out. Thrilled, I was not.

"Good for you! Hey, if you're free from watching your group later and if you can stand it, a few of us are going to get together after the kids are down for the night."

"Maybe, if I don't throw myself in the fire first."

"Picnic table past the canoe shed." Marissa turned and hurried away.

As Caleb shyly made his way over, Marissa passed him and ran her fingers through his blond hair. Coming forward, Caleb was smiling from ear to ear and I noticed

Marissa pause, look at her hand, and then dust it off. While Marissa walked away, she kept curiously peering back over her shoulder. I'm not sure what she was glancing for, but perhaps she feared I might take off, leaving Caleb all alone to fend for himself.

I drew another deep breath and quickly gave myself a pep talk. I can do this. I can put up a front. I can do this. I do it every day.

"So, you're into this marshmallow thing are you?"

Caleb graciously grinned, "Never had a roasted one before."

"Well then. What's your name?" I inquired, but despised asking because we shared the same cabin and I've had to call his name a few times at bed check.

"Caleb."

"Mr. Caleb, I'm Gavin. I guess we should go see what is going down over by the fire."

For the next half hour, I squatted on the ground patiently instructing Caleb how to roast the perfect marshmallow. I have to admit it was fun and Caleb and I both laughed hysterically when a marshmallow melted off the stick and plopped down onto the coals, sizzling at the bottom of the fire. It was very offbeat spending time with a young kid, something I'd never done before. It struck me that Caleb was having the time of his life when he positioned his tiny frail arm on my shoulder.

#

One of my fellow trainees was staying in for the night, so after I helped settle the campers, I decided to accept Marissa's invitation. Near the storage shed, in the distance, a small fire burned and I could hear the dull chatter from those gathered. For a second I hesitated by the out-building, debating if I should continue forward. He was there. Right there, a short distance in front of me planted on the top of a picnic table; Jacob.

I whispered to myself, "Should've jumped in the fire."

I continued on, palms sweaty and the need to control the rhythm of my breathing. Thankfully, some of the others I had met earlier in the day were there too, so I wouldn't feel like a total tool approaching an arena of the unknown.

Without looking, I pitched up a greeting wave then gravitated to the fire, holding my hand out to the flames as if they were cold. Trying to look cool likely made me look like a complete idiot I'm sure, since it was seventy-five degrees outside. I couldn't exactly waltz over and thrust Jacob a high-five. Though it wasn't unnerving as what happened in the parking lot on the last day of school, the brief glance at each other was enough.

Seconds later, Marissa emerged at my side.

"Careful, you're getting very close to those third row five seats back." She joked in her caustic way.

"Couldn't decide if it was better to burn to death or jump in the lion's den."

"Nice show with the kid by the way."

"Is this grief or an observation?" My reply was mainly directed at her choice use of the word "show".

"Either way, your reputation's fate is still secure. No clones will likely be aware of any imprint of kindness." Marissa dug deeper with her lyrical prose. So, naturally I engaged.

"Since I'm left without a choice I can navigate through this summer, even if it's all a façade. Wouldn't be my first successful attempt at living up to others' expectations."

Something about the tone or the way Marissa coined her words stabbed in the side. She had a knack for calling out everything I believed she considered a flaw in myself. Sure, I had flaws, but who is exempt? Feeling judged and out of place, I didn't hang around the campfire gathering very long and I'm sure Marissa didn't buy the excuse I gave, that I was tired. For the first time ever in my life, I sensed what it must be like for an outsider.

When I returned to Cabin 7 all of the self-segregating boys were sound asleep. In my tiny bed, briefly, I reflected on the fireside chat with Marissa, but soon I drifted off and started dreaming about Taylor and Chloe sharing a banana split and strangely, Jayden and I were hiding underneath the table listening to their conversation. Considering the bizarre dream, maybe there was some vague truth in my excuse of being exhausted.

I felt a pitiful nudge and at first, I believed it was Jayden, part of my dream, until another hardy tug pressed at my side. Startled, I opened my heavy eyelids.

"What the," My eyes focused in, "Oh, what's up little guy?"

Caleb pranced at my bedside shielding his mouth then he leaned in, getting closer to my ear.

He whispered, "I have to go to the bathroom."

I dozed off and the voice, urgent, returned louder in my ear.

"Now!"

Alarmed into a panic, I jumped from the thin bed and Caleb began giggling. I wanted to cover his mouth so the other kids wouldn't wake up. Instead, I ushered him out of the cabin in a swift motion as he struggled with his hands clinging to his private area. Picturing the outcome of Caleb peeing in his pajamas gave me the urgency to sprint through the dark toward an avocado liberator.

Caleb entered the sixties bathroom as I leaned against

an exterior wall trying not fall asleep. I couldn't stop yawning. Following a couple stretches trying to keep myself alert and a few more yawns, I heard Caleb let out a whine from something painful. As horrible as it sounds, I rolled my eyes.

"You okay in there buddy?"

I hesitated then headed for the door so I could make sure he was all right. Just as I reached the door, it sprang open, almost smacking me in the face. Quickly, I maneuvered out of the way and I'm sure that some form of noise spewed from my mouth. When I glanced at Caleb, he started giggling at how stupid I must've looked dodging out of the way of the wooden door. I couldn't help but notice that both of Caleb's sunken cheeks had tiny tears sliding down his pale skin.

We shuffled back to the cabin, slid back in bed, but I couldn't fall back to sleep. I laid there for hours and a couple of times I got up, went outside, and walked around the exterior of the building.

The night was peaceful, only recognizable noises from bugs chirping and random hoots from an owl perched on a branch overhead, but inside my turbulent mind, a violent storm was brewing. Being upset with my father for making me be here combined with the elevated uneasiness I felt in Marissa's presence had me reeling. And the Jacob situation added a level of intensity too. A violent game of tackle was called for and I was unclear if I wanted to attack or act as the tackling dummy.

I could swear the sun was coming up when I finally began falling asleep. There was no way of checking since there was no clock around and I preferred not waking the kids by trying to fish around for my wristwatch in my bag. Clocks and I were becoming enemies.

Worse than the sound of an early mechanical buzz was the pattering of ten young boys, thrilled and springing to life, especially since I had slept three hours at the most.

…just some kid.

From a small pond, murky brown water lapped against the dock anchors as the campers prepared for a swimming lesson. Trying my best I assisted wherever I sensed the need when really what I wanted to do was convince the staff that the disgusting water was rather unsafe and there had to be something else we could do, like sleep. The counselor I shadowed found absolutely no humor in my suggestion. He was far too serious in his position for my taste.

From what I observed of the kids' appearance it seemed as though they couldn't afford catching anything viral or bacterial from a pond filled with contaminated looking water. I wondered if they even knew how to swim, but the counselors were unconcerned and assured me that most of the children could reach the bottom with their feet, which was a good thing for me because the thought of having to jump into that mud-hole and save someone revolted me. I reminded them that people had drowned in a tablespoon of water, but I still found no comedic relief within the tightly wound.

Hearing the shuffling dirt from behind I sensed someone approaching and when she tapped on my shoulder, I knew straight away, to whom the fingers belonged. Marissa's touch held the same impudent nature as her cynical remarks.

Breathe. I reminded myself to breathe.

Marissa crouched beside me, "I need a hand."

I turned to face her, "No problem, what's up?"

"Your admirer refuses to let anybody else help him with his vest. Must be a guy thing." Marissa shrugged.

Remaining collected, I responded, "You help a kid

with marshmallows and you're a buddy for life."

"Might be hope for you yet."

Marissa disappeared for a few minutes and returned playfully tugging Caleb by a loop adorning a PFD. His personal flotation device was bright yellow. No doubt, he wouldn't get lost in a crowd and there was no way the vivid color could be camouflaged within the muddy water of the small pond.

I inched forward, "Mr. Caleb, Mr. Caleb. With this vest you're going to look like a little yellow duck and once you hit the water you can go quacky, quacky, quacky." I said, thinking if only my friends could see me now and hear how completely absurd I sounded.

Grinning, Caleb added, "You're wacky, wacky, wacky."

Caleb was set and about to jump in the water as I reached over, ruffling his delicate hair. Caleb leaned forward, jumped, and plunged into the water. Perplexed, I turned facing Marissa.

Holding out my hand I said, "This is too much."

A tuft of blond hair rested in my palm.

"Sad."

I brushed off my hand, "What causes that? What's wrong with him?"

Marissa's eyes shifted, "Let's not talk about it."

The clarity of what happened the night before hit home. Remembering Marissa brushing her hands, looking back toward Caleb with a sort of sadness and recalling the sounds of his pain in the bathroom cut through me. Caleb was sick and so were the other kids. That was what the summer camp was all about and those facts hadn't truly registered with me until that very moment. I mean, I understood, yet it seemed so fictional. But seeing it, feeling it, touching it, rang the bell.

#

Pecking away at my lunch, Taylor crossed my mind and I thought about the great time she was probably having in Mexico. Her parents dug me and I could've taken the trip with them and that was the plan we'd put together during Christmas break, but when my dad caught wind of our arrangement, he shut it down faster than the Department of Transportation closes a bridge during an ice storm. It wasn't the cost because he wasn't required to pay for anything either since Taylor's parents had offered the trip as a Christmas gift for both of us. Her parents were going to be there as well and I would've had a room to myself, but that wasn't satisfactory enough for him. Along with his other short answers to my requests, that time with his typical "no" he added a couple of new words — child support. Besides, unbeknown to me at the time, Dad had plans to the contrary. At least I believe he must've known what he wanted me to do for the summer or at least the plan was in the works.

While pressing green peas onto the prongs of a plastic fork, my random thoughts shifted to Chloe and her ritual summer diet. If she wanted to diet and could stay away from the marshmallow pit, I should suggest she volunteer her services to "Life Me Up" for one summer. Either the food or one gulp from the rancid watering hole might assist her in the seasonal quest for a banging body. I smirked at the notion, because knowing Chloe she would have bags of candy hidden in a compartment of her luggage.

By now, Austin's visitation with his grandmother in Texas was well underway where he was brushing up on his twang and storing up stories about the many cowgirls he conquered during his stay. It was a sickening visual but

I imagined a tiny girl wearing a cowboy hat, holding a lasso and hugging a Redwood tree.

At a football retreat somewhere, Jayden was likely pounding flesh in the hot summer sun and noting the several different recruiters who approached begging him to apply to whatever college they represented. His tall-tales I was more apt to believe. While most teenage boys spend vast amounts of vigor focused on girls, Jayden directed his energy to football. I believed his obsession, his drive, was unhealthy. The protein shakes, the workouts, studying plays, and a calendar to keep up with it all were a bit maddening.

My eyes sunk heavy with tiredness; my thinking dwindled to the awareness of nothing more than the sounds of the eating area.

The dining hall was so stuffy that in my stupor I felt a vague draft wave across my face from where a female counselor had rushed in through a side door. Taking a deep breath, my eyelids lifted a measurable amount as my eyes traced her steps as she hurried across the dining hall. I hadn't noticed that Jacob was there until he urgently stood up from a table, followed the girl rushing across the room, and out the side door.

Lunch wasn't happening so I discarded the leftovers in the trash and headed back to my cabin. Since there were a couple of hours of downtime before the counselor I shadowed needed my assistance, I wanted to squeeze in a short nap. I was so exhausted I figured the heat in the cabins wouldn't bother me much since nodding off in the dining hall was easy enough.

Yawning took over before I was half of the way back to the cube of cabins. Things were rather quiet for the middle of the afternoon, or so I believed, until I circled around the corner of Cabin 12. All of the kids and instructors that were normally buzzing around the encampment stood congregated on the other side of the notorious bathroom facility. Then as I inched closer to Cabin 7, an emergency vehicle was backing up diagonally to the right of the crowd. Shortly after it stopped, paramedics rushed around carrying various types of medical equipment.

I quickened my pace, getting closer, and noticed Marissa positioned near the rear of the gawkers. Just ahead, a couple of paramedics forced a noisy metal gurney forward as several counselors motioned for the younger children to head in a certain direction away from the commotion.

Reaching Marissa's side I questioned, "What happened?"

Nibbling on a fingertip, Marissa eased backwards, "Don't know, but it can't be good."

The gurney exited the cabin and a stark-white sheet hid a small lump spanning half the length of the stretcher. I lifted up to my toes for a better view as Marissa spun around, covering her eyes.

"Oh my God." Distress owned her voice.

"Are they…"

I hadn't finished my sentence and Marissa didn't hesitate getting out of there. No goodbye, see you later, nothing. I didn't blame her and I did the same.

The entire afternoon was an eerie one at Lift Me Up. Counselors carried on with their schedules as best they could considering the gloomy atmosphere. Children were crying, counselors were distraught, and efforts to seize the day grew hopeless. There was more than one reason for the children to be upset. Not only were they acquainted with the deceased, each of those underage campers knew first hand that it could have been them riding away that day, dead or alive. Those were the hard facts they lived with daily. For some of them, their whole life had been that way.

Death had never reached my life up until then and how to handle it wasn't exactly second nature. The situation fueled the anxiety I thought had finally settled in. I needed to talk with someone about it. It wasn't easy, though after rounding up some change and a few calls later, I managed to get Taylor on the phone.

"Yes, like a dead body!"

"OMG! How did they die?"

"Not sure."

"Just try to hang in there. It will be over soon."

"Couldn't be soon enough for me."

"Listen, I got to go, we were on our way out and my parents are waiting for me."

The call came close to being nearly as short as the conversation with my dad several days back. I have a tragedy happening and her parents couldn't wait one damn minute? No one likes to talk about death, just as with Taylor, all anyone wants to discuss are the basics. Where did it happen? How did they die? Followed with, everything will be all right or will be over soon. I pushed back the feelings I had about the day, because that's what I do.

Resulting from the emotional stress I guessed, all the young campers slipped into bed extra early. Later, I along with other trainees was gathered by the bonfire listening to one of the guys strumming his guitar. I sat resting on the ground tossing bits of dried grass on the fire, bored out of my mind, and still distraught that Taylor couldn't speak with me longer. I mean, how many times had I listened to her ramble on about a bad haircut and she didn't have time for me after someone had died?

Marissa parked on the ground next to me, "Hey."

"How goes it?"

"Sorry about your little friend."

Aloof in my response, "No need to apologize to me, he was just some kid."

Not the reaction I expected, but Marissa stormed to her feet. Her motions were exaggerated, desperate even, and because of the commotion, Jacob, who was nearby, glanced upward.

Angrily storming away, Marissa shouted, "Wow, you really are a heartless bastard!"

My response sounded harsher than its intentions. I held no attachments to someone that I'd just met, I can say with honesty. There was no call for an apology in that regard. Expressing my feelings by referring to Caleb as just some kid was simply a bad choice of wording. Setting the record straight was important enough to me so I went after Marissa.

As I neared the canoe shed, Marissa reached the top of a knoll veering off through a grouping of trees. I almost caught up with her, watching her enter a chocolate-brown building. The door was shutting just as I reached to heave it open. Marissa stood paused in the middle of the room, her back facing the door.

"Listen, I didn't mean…"

Not letting me finish, she abruptly shifted around and eased closer, nearly invading my personal space.

"Just some kid?"

She paused and I, feeling uncomfortable, guilty, jetted my eyes around the room waiting for more of her venom.

"Despite your ego, you're also just some kid. I'm just some kid," her anger mounted, "he was somebody, he was someone's child, brother and a grandson."

Though I wished to explain myself, Marissa's dig spun my intent to a defensive stance and patience escaped me.

"Hey, I just met the kid, what, two weeks ago?" I took a few steps backward for some breathing room.

"Right, no reason to see him as a human being with feelings. But he is dead, he doesn't have any feelings right! Just another dead kid!"

Marissa rammed forward grazing me with her shoulder, sprinted through the room and out of the building. I didn't see any sense in chasing after her again. The results would've been the same; another argument, more misunderstanding, more innuendo, and more aggression coming from a girl who obviously loathed my clones and me.

Resentment surged in my voice, "Drama. This is sure going to help me be a well-rounded young man. Thanks Dad."

The day was not done and nor were the theatrics as Jacob entered through the door behind me. His voice was memorable, distinct and his words accented as if he were professionally trained to speak in such a way. It's both intimidating and unnerving, although familiar, like home.

"Everything alright in here?"

I almost whispered, "Couldn't be better."

Jacob strolled in front of me and sat on top of a table. A feather ran the length of my spin.

Jacob spoke calmly, "Oh, things could always be better."

"I can't say anything right with that girl."

"Maybe it's your perception of what's right that's off."

Not him too. Defense took position for the next play.

I popped back, snapping my head upward, "Yeah, whatever that means!"

"Did you say what you feel or did you speak words in order to live up to your image?"

Jacob remained collected, but not me. Immediately the past was meeting the future in the present and I was in two places at one time.

"What caused you to become so righteous? You know how it is. Have you forgotten that your feet have walked the same halls that I've walked? It's brutal."

He knew damn well what I meant or at least I expected him to.

Jacob added, "Only if you allow it to affect you that way. How you react is what's important."

"Hey buddy, don't act as if you were always this," I motioned my hand from the top to the bottom of Jacob's body, "this, whatever it is!"

My heart raced and Jacob continued in the calm. He wasn't going to engage in the way I felt though I wanted him to. If he could experience each emotion that I had felt every fall, winter, and spring morning for two years then he would understand.

"She had a death in her family recently."

Confused because my past hadn't caught up with my present I asked, "What are you talking about?"

"Marissa. She just moved here."

It became clear that Marissa was upset about someone else's departure and not completely troubled by my haphazard statement alone. My accelerant merely fueled a fire.

"Ah, well how was I supposed to know?"

"I bet you know what kind of shoes she was wearing

the first time you saw her."

"I mean Jacob, really?"

Jacob lifted his shoulders, "Just saying."

"Yeah, well save it for all your gloomy friends dressed in black!"

"Point taken."

"Judgment isn't some market that the in crowd has cornered you know."

"Right. The only market that's cornered is that of alienating." Jacob suggested.

I knew he had it in him and he was ready to go there.

"Did I alienate you or did you do that to yourself? I recall you wearing the same shoes once!"

"Another point taken." Jacob remained collected.

"If you think that I don't know we're basically all the same, believe me I know! Who can explain the natural order of things? I can't. From the time we hit the playground it's a battle to see who is going to be at the top of the monkey bars!"

"And that battle continues through life. Look at the state of the world. Wars, people starving, the homeless. It is only an extension of what started in the first grade. Just bigger kids with the power to pull a bigger trigger." Jacob's voice was smooth, sincere, and caring.

"Well, you tell me how to escape it."

"Still trying to figure that out. I may not save the world, but I don't want to be part of the problem."

I lightly chuckled, "What saved you, since you insist that you're not a self-created hoax?"

"I get how you could say that. It was this place. In the summer after ninth grade. Changed my whole perception."

"Yeah? How is that?"

Jacob gazed off reflecting, "Can't explain it really. I

just realized that there are more important things than myself."

"Noble, but walking around as an outcast isn't going to change the world." I pointed toward his shoes.

"Again, that's just your perception. You ever think that the crowd dressed in black observes you and the other makers of teenage protocol as the outcast?"

I shot back, "No, I don't. I see them trying to fit in."

"Some, sure. Some don't have the means to do so for whatever reason. Money, social skills. Besides, who wants to be remembered as the guy who always had on the right shoes?"

"Okay, I'll give you that."

"In the process, we've all failed in getting to truly know each other."

"Right, like, I truly thought I knew you." My sorrowful voice was revealing.

"Gavin, I'm the same person. I've grown. I've experienced different things, but I'm still the same person."

"Yeah, you look it." I kidded.

"Cold."

"Call it what you want. I don't get it."

"That's the beauty of it all. You shouldn't have to."

Jacob jumped to his feet and in his artistic way, sauntered over to a bulletin board on the wall. He removed a piece of artwork, came over, and handed it to me.

"Read this."

My heart could've stopped right in the moment and I would've been okay with that. A sinking feeling came over me and I felt like I was drowning, but drowning from too much air. My lungs expanding faster than I'd known was possible. The room seemed bigger and smaller at the same time. My palms were slippery and it felt that I was out of the space called time.

Below a picture of trees, a house, and a swing-set, words were written in crayon that would be etched in my heart forever.

My name is Caleb. I'm eight. My dad is a firefighter. My mom takes care of me. IF I grow up, I want to be like Gavin, he is awesome.

My voice strained, "Too much."

I had to sit down. I did and Jacob sat beside me resting his arm across my shoulders. The feather again.

I could hardly get the words out, "W-h-y me?"

"Doesn't matter why you. What matters and what you should remember is, you grew up. There was no IF when you were eight years old."

I was torn, crippled, and I felt like an asshole.

"I couldn't imagine."

Jacob moved closer, "That's two of us."

"Is it wrong that I have mixed feelings?"

"Mixed as in?" Jacob questioned.

"I just met the kid. I mean, it's sad that he died, but I'm not torn up about it. If anything I'm more twisted about the words on that paper."

"At least you're honest Gavin. Suppose that's natural. Count yourself lucky."

"How's that? Lucky that I'm an insensitive bastard?"

"That's not true. I say lucky because you hadn't spent much time with Caleb. I understand how you feel. Had something similar happen to me." Again, Jacob reflected.

"Yeah?"

"Yeah, but I had more time, got attached. I don't see myself as unlucky though. Blessed. Blessed that I shared a moment in time with someone beautiful. Don't get me wrong, I was mad at the world. Clarity comes when it comes."

"And you turned into a goblin." I joked.

Jacob shoved me off the table.

…the wrong information.

Understandably, for the next few days, Marissa and I sidestepped each other, or that is what I was doing anyway. I knew I should man-up and attempt to explain myself or at least try to come to some resolution for the rift between us. If anything came out of it at all, at the least we might agree to disagree. We were two out of seven billion people and not everyone is destined to get along. Like Jacob said, look at the state of the world.

My duties concluded for the day and I discovered Marissa down in the field where the archery activities carried out. I watched as she drew back the string on a bow. Releasing the string, the arrow soared in an arch across the sky and plunged into the target. Marissa completed the procedure as though she'd done it many times before.

She situated her students and assisted them putting their hands in the proper positions, plant a proper stance, then she eased backward. At that point, I seized the opportunity to approach as I inhaled long deep breaths. Marissa's eyes looked toward me, and quickly darted away.

"Can we call a truce?" I asked politely.

"Are we at war?"

I couldn't get a read from the inflection in her question.

"Don't know, but this avoiding thing is so old school. If that's what we're doing?"

Marissa inched closer, "Sometimes old school is the way to go, depending on the mood."

"Listen, I'm sorry. I, I, I'm just not good at stuff like this. It was wrong for me to say what I said-the way I said it." I had to break the ice somehow and usually an apology was the way to go, I guessed.

"I'm sorry I got bent out of shape. This whole damn situation has triggered some feelings that I'd rather go away."

"I just shove them way back in my mind in a dark place."

"Scary place. Got one myself."

I was unsure where the conversation might go after that. Would we make confessions or end up in another game of wrong word choice? Thankfully, Jacob entered the picture just in time, as far as I was concerned.

"Good to see all the rows commingling." Jacob smirked.

"Ah, somebody has been discussing my conversations," I replied.

Jacob reached out tapping my shoulder, "Oh come on, you're used to it."

"Am I really that bad?" Tones of concern filled my question.

"No. It's just the surface dirt, but fret ye not, we can wash it off in the loo." Jacob kidded.

Marissa grimaced at the two of us strangely.

"The two of you are sort of like those two from that movie," she snapped her fingers, "uh, Thelma and Louise."

"As long as I get to be Thelma." I said as serious as I could.

Jacob argued, "Hey wait a minute now."

"Oh, now you're going to fight over the part you play?" Marissa questioned.

Suddenly, I felt overly self-conscious. "Okay, now seriously. Am I that bad?"

Jacob folded his arms across his chest, "Not sure what to say Gavin. I try not to judge. It's your journey."

Marissa jumped in. "Spoiled. Narcissistic. Pompous. Self-absorbed."

She said it so inimically; I grew agitated. "Okay! You're not one to hold back."

"Too much for your ego?" Marissa dug in her claws like a lion tearing apart its prey.

My defensiveness ramped up, "Well, what about you?"

Marissa's tone was stern. "What about me?"

"Dark. Gloomy. Depressed. Loathing. Should I go on?"

"I didn't know we were talking about me. You asked the question." Marissa retorted.

It boiled. That first bubble rose to the top of the scorching water.

"How is it that you people…"

Head snapping to one side, Marissa interrupted, "You people?"

"What?" I was confused.

"You know, there's no hope for you." The girl in black turned and stormed away.

Shouting at both Marissa and Jacob I said, "That's it. Do your thing. Run off like a pampered drama queen. Issues! See, see, I can't say anything right!"

Jacob unwrapped his arms, "Wow, that conversation went to the can quickly."

Explosively I barked, "Who can have a conversation with someone who can't stay present past six words? Did I scamper away with my tail hidden between my legs after she said all those vile things about me?"

Jacob's voice stayed relaxed and controlled, "We should go find her. We'll all take a deep breath, count to ten and try to find common ground. What do you think?"

"Right now…I don't know. Whatever! I don't know anymore! Never had to deal with something like this. You lead the way. I'm done! I don't want to be the leader anymore."

In an instant, I was free. Like someone snapped his or her fingers, giving permission. For so long, for so many years I had stood in front leading the troops, preparing the plans and authoritatively delegating others to execute the agenda.

As early as I could remember they followed behind mimicking my moves like a game of Simon Says. Even my emotions set the tone of the day. If I wished for everyone to be in a great mood, I portrayed a great mood; it didn't even have to be authentic.

With all the admiration, I would place the bet that not one of them could announce my favorite color if they were called to do so. Set the stakes as high as you wish.

What Marissa expressed was the truth. Like I had confessed, I know what I'd become, but it stung realizing that someone like her, or Jacob for that matter, could see right through to my own beliefs about myself. My outward expression had become an addiction, a drug I couldn't live without. The outside was destroying the inside and my core was set in motion to have faith in an exterior, which was nothing but a lie. That person, who opened his mouth, speaking thoughtless words, wasn't me. I was hiding; hiding in the corner of a cell, screaming for someone to set me free.

If Taylor had only given me the time when I phoned earlier…

#

Searching for Marissa turned up nothing by the time Jacob and I met back up at the canoe shed.

"Any luck?" I asked.

Jacob leaned against the outbuilding and flicked a wedge of hair from his face, "I looked everywhere."

For a second I paced around in a circle kicking the sandy dirt when something dawned on me.

"What about the bathrooms? Girls spend most of their lives in there."

Jacob sprang from the wall, "Bathroom!"

We darted up a rock-covered hill, weaving through a small row of pine trees heading to one of the two girls' restrooms on the campgrounds. Jacob hesitated before delicately tapping on the door.

Marissa's familiar voice said, "Someone is in here."

"Marissa, it's Jacob."

"What do you want?"

"You okay?"

She spoke softly, "I'm fine."

Jacob tilted his head closer to the door, "You want to talk?"

As though she was hiding under a blanket, her answer was distant, "Not really, go away."

Agitation festered, so I stepped forward and pounded on the door. Jacob's mild manner was just not working for me.

"Marissa, if you don't come out here I'm coming in." I sounded as patient as my father.

"Smooth! Would you relax?" Jacob snarled in a whispered.

"I mean really, is it going to make any difference? She already thinks I'm table gum."

Jacob flicked his hair and his brow lifted, "Table gum?"

"You know, people put used gum underneath tables?"

"How original."

"Was, now everybody uses it," once more banging on the door, "Marissa!"

Surely, Marissa hoped we would leave her alone. I waited a couple of minutes, observing Jacob, who looked like he had a running debate streaming inside his mind, then I decided to take the risk and enter.

"I'm going in."

"Not sure you should. Maybe we should stay calm and wait till she comes out."

"Cut it with that shit Jacob, she's a girl. Could be hours."

"Think before you speak." Jacob suggested.

Rolling my eyes at him, I heaved the bathroom door open and stepped inside. I didn't see Marissa; I concluded she had to be in one of the stalls.

Four stalls lined the lime-green walls and because of the scarce lighting, I couldn't clearly see which one of them was occupied. I pressed ahead, I had come this far, I wasn't stopping now.

Hoping and praying there was only one person in the bathroom, I approached each stall with caution, glancing downward at the floor through the small space at the bottom of each partition seeking signs of life. I cleared the first stall, on to the second, nothing, the third, nothing, and then to the last remaining stall. With each passing compartment, the light faded.

Reaching the last section, my focus adapted to the changing shadows caused by the movement of my body. When I stooped over, a pair of legs rested curled on the floor, a hand off to the side and sending me into a panic state, a blood smeared shard of glass.

Charging as though I were on a football field during a game I whirled around, headed for the exit as quickly as I could. Jacob was still on the outside pacing back and forth, where I chattered at him with great force and distress as I was running off in the direction of the woods.

"Jacob! I'm going for help. She tried to kill herself!"

"What!" Jacob spun and headed for the bathroom entrance.

Not knowing whom to seek out, I dashed straight for Sarah's office. Never in the most important games had I ever sprinted so fast. When I reached the office, my overflowing emotions caused my words to delay, to come across in a frenzy.

Breathing heavy, I blurted, "Someone is hurt, we need help!"

Sarah trailed me out the door. Surprising me, she had no problem keeping up as we sprinted through the campground. I even chose shortcuts that required jumping down a small incline and thrusting over rotting timber from where a tree had fallen, but Sarah kept right in step.

As we ran, I explained what little I knew and I'm not sure it made any sense to her. I mentioned floor, glass, bathroom, and suicide; basically whatever came out, came out. That much I remembered expressing between the winded panting.

Jacob was waiting outside the bathroom as Sarah headed straight inside without saying anything.

Shaken, and guilt ridden, I desperately questioned, "Is she okay? Please tell me she is not dead!"

Jacob placed an arm on the upper part of my back. I didn't like it. I expected the delivery of bad news. My breath smothered me and once again, space became larger and smaller at the same time.

"Let's go for a walk." Jacob suggested.

I shifted and yanked myself from underneath Jacob's heavy arm.

"No! You tell me she is okay! You tell me she is okay! Jacob, she is okay, right?"

Jacob leaned in closer, placing both hands on each of

my shoulders as his head tilted forward.

"No! You say it! No. No! This is not cool! No!"

Even If he wanted to, Jacob couldn't say anything because of my hysteria. I had to say that I'd preferred he not speak either because if he did, whatever he said was final. Like she was dead. Briskly, I took two steps backward letting Jacob's hands fall; I split and headed for a touchdown.

Jacob shouted, "Gavin wait!"

I ran. Ran hard without any idea where I was heading. When I reached the pond, I could not breathe. I gasped for air. I parked my sweaty hands on my head and then I waved them at my sides. I pivoted and circled, bent over and momentarily lost my bearings.

I heard Jacob heavily panting as he caught up with me.

"Gavin, listen to me," Jacob said while taking deep breaths, "She is not dead!"

Frustrated I asked, "Why didn't you say something?"

"We were right outside the door and I didn't want her to hear us talking about it. It's insensitive."

My hysteria transformed to a nervous laughter.

"Insensitive? Really now? Tiptoeing around a crazy person won't make any difference will it? Will it make them more of a lunatic?"

Nothing from Jacob. Silence. Except for his breathing.

Pressing my hands to my face I bellowed, "Why is this happening to me?"

Breathing heavily Jacob retorted, "Are you really saying this right now? What is happening to you Gavin?"

"Yes. I am. What is happening to me? I've been thrown into this chaos. Kids dying! People trying to do themselves in, over what, some silly misunderstanding? I'm not stoked about this at all!"

"Gavin, would you just listen to yourself? What about what was happening to the kid before he passed away? Are you even thinking about that? Leukemia, Gavin. No picnic you know. It's vile. And do you have any idea what these kids have to go through every day of their lives? Do you have any notion of what it's like to know that you are dying?"

"Back to me being the bad guy. I get it Jacob. I understand what the kids are going through. I mean, I guess I never thought about it, not until it was right in my face. But, but what about this girl? My incorrect choice of words causes someone to hide in a bathroom stall and…"

Seething Jacob responded, and he stopped me from speaking as he flung his arms in the air.

"Oh come on! Don't give yourself the credit to have that power over someone! Anyway, she didn't try to kill herself!"

"Unless I'm truly going crazy, I saw what I saw."

Jacob calmed, "It's not what you thought."

"Well, I for the second time today, am at a loss for the politically correct words to use and my fashion focused mind is limited to what images it can observe and translate the meaning." By the last word, I was directly in Jacob's personal space.

"Just calm down."

"I'm calm," I inhaled a deep breath and exhaled as I retreated, "Now, tell me what I didn't see."

"Marissa is a cutter." Jacob's eyes focused on the ground.

"A cutter? Got me. What's a cutter?"

"She cuts herself."

"Well yeah. Obvious. She wasn't in there designing jewelry."

Irritated Jacob said, "No. Not cut like you're thinking."

"Are you purposely trying to wind me up?"

"A cutter, Gavin. How can you not know this? Let me think." Jacob paused, "A cutter is not attempting to end their life when they cut. They cut or inflict pain upon themselves as a coping mechanism. That's about all I know about it. Usually triggered when they're upset. Under some emotional distress."

"That's just weird."

"Maybe so. People do what they do. Some drink, some smoke, some drug, some cut, and some overdo. Some hide behind clothing," Jacob motioned at himself, "Some hide behind a vamped up exterior," He motioned at me, "a lot of the time, all efforts to cope. You'll have to do your own research. I'd rather not feed you the wrong information."

"Deep."

Jacob flipped his hair, "Complicated, complex, confused world."

…pleasure and the pain.

At first, it struck me as odd that every time I had seen Marissa since day one she consistently wore long-sleeved shirts even though it was summer. She was hiding pain in a compartment in the background and hiding the battle scars on her wrist underneath a length of cloth.

Privately, Sarah conferred with me with regard to the subject of cutting. I listened with an open mind, but I couldn't get my head around the facts. I understood the basics; I still thought it was weird. Like Jacob said, every person has his or her own way of dealing with their life circumstances.

Since Marissa and I hadn't gotten much further along than our battle of words, Jacob filled me in on the details. I felt I was missing fragments of the puzzle while trying to understand what seemed to be Marissa's sole purpose in life and that was to confront me. Maybe this is the perfect example for what Jacob meant when he said, "We've all failed to truly know each other."

Marissa wasn't attacking me personally, but responding to my harsh words and my abrasive attitude. In a way, I was guilty as hell, but in a way, I wasn't. Certain phrases taken out of context, combined with what she was personally going through created the workings for a huge explosion. I was the spark to the fuse, I concluded.

Similar to my dad, Marissa's father had suffered serious financial setbacks when the markets crashed. Some people are better at handling extreme pressure, but for some, the turmoil colliding with other internal issues already present might lead to complete devastation.

My father bounded in one direction, became financially conservative while rethinking his entire value structure.

From what I gathered, his losses were nothing compared to what Marissa's father had experienced. At no fault of Marissa's father, he lost everything. He just happened to have his investments at the top of the list when the economy began calling names and collapsing inward.

Tragically, Marissa's father leapt in a direction that unfortunately ended his life leaving her with scars that weren't the results of a shard of glass. My abrasive nonchalant attitude served about as much good as applying ammonia to an open wound.

Understandably, Marissa was embarrassed and she remained out of sight for few days. She didn't come around me anyway. Jacob remained in contact with her; all the while assuring her there was no need to avoid me. He put it mildly — we all have problems. I, for sure wouldn't argue with the truth. I had seen the man in the mirror.

"I'm so humiliated." Marissa expressed.

"Don't be. Trust me, underneath that eggshell exterior is a good person."

When Jacob finished telling me about their conversation I wanted to slug him for suggesting my exterior was eggshell. It was harder than that I promised, jokingly. Later in the week, Jacob persuaded Marissa to join the nightly bonfire below the canoe shed.

That night, I shared one of my many football tales with the other counselors in training. Captivating my audience, I visually expressed how my team once created this silly two-step routine to use in between plays in the hopes it would rattle the opposing team. As imaginable, our cocky display failed miserably and only fueled the rage of the offensive line who went on to slaughter us. Both a mental and physical annihilation of the highest order. Solidifying my story, I showed them the nasty scar from the wound I received during that game. Did I mention we lost?

"It hurt like hell, but it was the funniest thing ever."

Closing my tall tale, Jacob and Marissa arrived to save me from needing to tell another animated story. True to form, I had my spectators under my spell. What could I say? It came naturally and I'm cursed with a gift, an ability that I am unable to articulate. What I needed was a lesson on how to channel the talent into something creative or worthwhile in my life.

"S'up guys?" Jacob situated himself on the picnic table in his artful way.

Looking uncomfortable, Marissa eased down to the ground next to the fire. No one other than Jacob, Sarah and me knew what transpired in that bathroom. I wanted to put Marissa at ease, so I reminded myself of Jacob's advice, to think before I spoke. I would say prayed, but it was more as if I begged to some place higher as I joined her by the fire. I remained silent, afraid to speak.

Kindly, Marissa broke the silence, "You can talk. I won't break."

"You okay?"

"Yes. No."

Not able to face her just yet, I agreed, "Same here."

Marissa reached into a backpack retrieving a picture and then passed it to me.

"That's my family."

Marissa had awareness that Jacob informed me about the sordid details of her past and most likely, he had shared some fragments of mine. For him to play peacekeeper, I surmised it was necessary, which confirmed the theories of his gallant personality.

"Would you like to hear about them?"

"Sure, sorry I just don't want to say something wrong."

I hoped this might explain my non-response to the portrait. I was attentive enough to recognize that Marissa introduced the portrait and asked the question as an icebreaker or as a means to engage a conversation since I was reluctant to speak.

"It's okay Gavin, really it's not you."

"It's hard to tell."

"I'm having a tough time dealing."

"Do you want to share?"

"You remember talking about your dad, the economy, and those hedge funds?"

I vividly remembered, "First day. Yeah."

"Well, my dad didn't see the light. He jumped head on into the darkness."

"I..." I paused, "I know. I'm so sorry to hear that."

Jacob hopped from the picnic table, and came over wedging between us, his arms draped around our shoulders.

"Are we a happy family again?"

"Yes Louise." I kidded.

"Good Thelma, because I got an idea."

"Oh God." Marissa's eyes rolled.

Like recovering addicts, Marissa and I were trying to make it through one day at time while Jacob was planning a future. From the evidence collected over the past few weeks, I couldn't imagine how he ever concluded that a future even existed. Not with the three of us anyhow. Jacob was hopelessly optimistic that way. I wished I could say the same for myself since in light of all that had happened I was utterly terrified of using an improper adjective and summoning a full throttle meltdown. I would need to continue to condition myself to behave as Jacob suggested — think before I speak.

My past, my past's future, and my present were all colliding at the same time, in one place, directly in my face.

Jacob and Marissa sensed the same in some ways too I suppose; how could they not?

In my life, never again would I underestimate a deck of cards. No matter how many times someone shuffled the stack, the cards broken; the deck is always loaded in the universe's favor. It brings comfort knowing that within what comes off as chaos, there's order even though sometimes the method makes no sense at all.

What I learned was how quickly life and the world could amend in an instant, with no cautions at all. Every moment hinging on a scale that might weigh to one side or the other and all it takes to tip the balance is a small grain of sand. One flick of a switch. One earthquake. One death. Photographs becoming memories.

Wading through the quicksand at first left a notion that there would never be a connection between Marissa and myself, but somehow through the trials we had unearthed some common ground. I deduced that you can keep digging yourself a deeper hole or you can decide to put down the shovel. Then and only then might you find your way out of a stifling cavern for the healing fresh air available on the surface.

By the bonfire that night was our first good laugh at our problems, at life, at our egos, and mostly at ourselves.

Our remaining days at "Life Me Up", when we were not busy with the campers, we spent our free time together. A refreshing change of pace indeed.

…Camp Lift Me Up.

Jacob had one leg in the canoe and his other leg planted on the shore, while Marissa and I braced ourselves for the push-off.

"Bro, you're going to tip us over." I gripped the sides tighter trying to balance myself.

"I've got this." Jacob shoved with his land-based foot causing the canoe to shift across the water.

So, we were off floating across the mud-hole. Knowing my feelings about the swamp, I shouldn't have to mention this was not my idea.

"See, nothing to it."

"There are probably bodies weighted down on the bottom. Right underneath us even." I suggested.

"Gross." Marissa released her grip from the sides of the canoe.

Sitting, Jacob plunged a paddle in the water, "As long as they stay where they are and keep their limbs off the paddle it's all good."

"Oh great, now you've got me thinking about Camp Crystal Lake." Marissa centered herself in the middle of the canoe.

"Camp do who?" Jacob said.

I started making a noise, "Cha cha cha. Ha ha ha." A recognizable backing track of the scary movie Marissa was talking about.

Lifting his brow, Jacob recognized the tune, "Jason!"

Great, here we were in the middle of the pond, the sun was setting, and we were talking about a killer who at any minute could leap from the murky depths, snatch one of us and drag that unlucky person to a watery grave.

So fast, Jacob lunged forward taking a grip of my shirt

and I was caught so off guard, he had no problem tilting me over the edge of the canoe. How the two of them managed to stay on the rocking craft is anybody's guess.

Once I made it to the surface, I found both of them laughing hysterically.

"You know I'm going to kill you for this." I mentioned while wiping the filthy water from my face.

Just as quickly, with both hands, I latched onto the sides of the boat pulling downward using the weight of my body to heave upward. Easy enough, Jacob and Marissa hurled toward Jason's playground.

After giving them a few seconds to surface and catch their breath, I knew they were going to come after me, so I had no choice but to create a diversion.

"Oh my god, something just touched my foot!"

You've never seen three people move so fast.

Once we pulled ourselves from the grasp of Jason Voorhees, Marissa mentioned that the water was eating away at her fingernail polish, and that was a cue to hit the shower, like immediately. I'd kill Jacob later. I mean, that pollution removed nail varnish and it was on my penis! A boy and his penis are like a dog and his bone, no pun intended. Besides, I might need it someday, and really, who wanted to wind up in a medical office with some random doctor checking out the rash that's growing on your junk?

Water, clean water is so unappreciated. With this thought, I praised the avocado liberator and the showerhead-less bathing. Dare I mention that murky pond water stains undergarments forever?

#

But getting even was ever so sweet as they say.

Where there was fishing, there was bait. Where there was bait there might be crickets. Crickets we had.

Strategically, I positioned the plastic bag between the pillow and the pillowcase and returned it to Jacob's bed.

"Sweet dreams buddy."

#

And suddenly Camp Lift Me Up turned into The Prankster Games arena.

Jacob and I hunched behind a grouping of hemlocks to one side of a tamped trail that led from the archery area back to the square of buildings. With her classes just completed, Marissa was within our sights. At the right moment we bolted from our hiding spot and launched, a four can whip cream attack. She never saw it coming. She couldn't chase us because she couldn't see as she circled round and round similarly to someone trying to find a dangling piñata during a birthday party.

#

Somehow, the younger children talked us into joining in on a game of red-rover and watching us, as teenagers, trying to run through two small clamped hands without knocking one of the children down was a hilarious sight.

Just as that was over, Jacob and I settled at a picnic table and held a hotdog eating competition. Not a good idea! For this reason I would certainly never eat another frank for the rest of my life, I vomited for what seemed like twenty minutes. Even thinking about the smell of one cooking makes me nauseous.

I recovered quickly, which was good because a nearby farmer stopped by, dropping off more watermelons than the camp could ever use. He had obviously had a great harvest. Anyway, who could turn down fresh watermelon on a hot summer day?

I'm not sure who started it, but I certainly joined in when the first juicy piece of watermelon slapped the back of my neck. Shocking me, I saw the older counselors lighten up and engage in the battle. Watermelon was flying in every direction until there was no more solid ammunition, just mush, seeds and slime.

By then my hair was a shade of pink, I had a seed latched onto one of my eyebrows and one lodged in my ear canal. From the weight of the sticky liquid, Jacob's hair had gotten longer and its strands rested plastered along the front of his face. Marissa picked the wrong day to rebel and wear white, and the juices caused her dark eyeliner to stream downward, leaving her face looking like the rivers on a legend map. She was standing there laughing so hard she was crying.

With life, there would be tears and there will be laughter, but we would share the pleasure and the pain, together.

…alive at seventeen.

Like the clock on the school wall, time during the beginning of the summer seemingly stopped and unlike school, there wasn't an end of the period chime waiting to recommence the ticking hands.

Two years had sped along and the distance that had grown between Jacob and I got smaller that summer. The reconciliation was one of many blessings that occurred while I served time at a camp I didn't want to attend.

At the end of ninth grade during summer break while I was floating from city to city, bored enough to do push-ups while watching soap operas, Jacob attended Lift Me Up for the first time. Befriending an ailing child one year older than Caleb, Jacob was taken in after spending six incredible weeks with him. A short time following the end of the camp session that summer, Jacob lost an endearing person that he had grown to love. Immediately, following the trauma Jacob was thrown back to the rigors of high school life. The gift of a shiny collector car couldn't take away the pain of his loss. Undeniably, I had no idea of what he had gone through.

Back to that first day in the school parking lot where a ritual began, I recollected, if only I'd said something before Austin spoke or if I had pronounced something afterward, would things be different now? After all, Jacob had only changed on the outside. His despair masked with plaid and suspenders and eventually his style became a habit. In a way, it was a constant remembrance of one unforgettable moment in his life.

For the entirety of my life, I could beat myself up for my silent stance. I was Jacob's best friend and he was mine. Unlike most, Jacob even knew my favorite color. If there was possibly any meaning to it, my preferred choice from the crayon box was silver. Even though I loathed the arrival of a familiar sounding engine each morning, the color of the car I adored. And, too, I have to say that I adored the person behind the wheel.

Cowardly described my action for ignoring Austin's reckless ramblings and by not saying anything meant that I approved to some if only subconsciously. Even in his withdrawal from the status quo, Jacob could have reached out if he needed me and I would've been there, regardless, but grief clouded his thought processes just as ego clouded mine. At the time, I had no understanding of his transformation.

While the divide grew larger, Jacob thought I wouldn't have the aptitude for understanding or handling the way he chose to express himself. Meanwhile, on the other side of the cafeteria I concluded Jacob was disgusted at the sight of me. This mirroring of preconceptions has to be a common thread within the boundaries of the social scale.

A friendship decayed into nothingness and for two years I waited, waited for Jacob. All along Jacob was right in front of me hiding behind a triangular loaf of brown bangs, splotchy well-worn shoes and I took cover behind a personality that wasn't entirely me.

Eventually at camp in between the prankster wars, I broke down about Caleb's death. The emotion I suppressed finally made it through my cluttered mind.

From her prior observations, Marissa spent an hour explaining her earlier judgments about my actions from the minute I sat down on the old yellow bus until I bolted out of that chocolate-brown building. More importantly, her awareness of a helpless little boy admiring what he aspired to achieve if he lived a longer life. I had never thought about it until now, but Caleb could've passed as my little brother.

We both had bold blue eyes and our hair color was similarly blond. Maybe Caleb saw that too.

I'm sure that Caleb couldn't have known that I was a wreck, a coward or pretending to be an asshole, but what he saw was a dream. Caleb dreamt of growing up and becoming a man, though I was no man at all, except in his eyes. I stuck to what I'd said about not knowing him, not having an attachment, but it killed me thinking about what Caleb must've been going through and he saw me as a role model of sorts. At eight years old, Caleb knew he would never be like me — muscular, strong, independent and most of all, alive at seventeen.

Jacob was spot on when he pointed out how selfish my statements were as I whined and questioned why everything was happening to me.

As we rebuilt our relationship, it was refreshing to hear what Jacob had been doing since the day he put down a football and tuned into another world. I had no idea that I'd missed so many things in his life. I guess it was stupid and naive of me to think he was sitting at home alone and bored. There is an unspoken assumption that people at the lower end of the social order have no lives.

Jacob tried explaining his manner of dress, I still didn't get it, but at least I had learned that a tattered two-tone t-shirt, hole ridden Converse high-tops and roughly chopped hair doesn't represent the person behind the silver-rimmed glasses. The same could be said for whatever I elected to put on display as a representation of who I am as well.

Once the three of us had resolved our emotional confrontations and bonded, the hands of time regained momentum and service at Lift Me Up swiftly summed up. By the end of the season the weathered building that I had detested, grew to have character and the avocado green bathroom fixtures acquired a completely new meaning, mainly a reminder of Caleb. Him crying. His frailness. Him not present to finish out the summer, or a lifetime.

The night by the campfire when Jacob said, "Good, I have a plan," well, I still have my doubts, but I'm willing to try the experiment. Back home a tough crowd awaited. If we could pull it off…Well, we'll see.

#

The neglected yellow buses that I began calling antique, started leaving as soon as they campers filled them. For the trip back home, I was finally getting the chance to be a passenger in that Volkswagen that was all too familiar. On top of that, it was my favorite color!

Marissa's bus was ready to leave and waiting for her to board. Jacob, Marissa, and I paused, but there was nothing really left to say since we would see each other back home. Jacob had already told me that Marissa had moved to our area, but it was a surprise when I discovered she was attending the same school.

Marissa smiled inching closer, "There is only one thing left to do to solidify this crazy summer."

Marissa reached out, placed a strong grip on my shirt, and tore it down the center.

"Nice! Step one, Plan A." Jacob applauded.

I peered down at my ripped shirt, then toward Marissa, "Bet you wanted to do that a month ago."

Marissa stepped on the idling bus and waved goodbye. We wished we could ride together, but Jacob's car had another unique feature, it was a two-seater. Besides, Marissa preferred not depriving her mom of the thrill of meeting her at the big box retailer. Marissa had mentioned to Jacob and me that she thought her mother was extremely lonely since her father's passing and the trip home would give them a chance to catch up.

Just before departing, Jacob and I rushed over to Sarah's office for a second to tell her goodbye where I apologized for being such a tool on the first day and thanked her for helping me understand a subject that I knew nothing about. She invited me back and I told her I would consider it, but I couldn't make any promises. She thanked me for sticking it out and then said I seemed lighter for whatever that was worth.

Turned out that I'd grown quite fond of Sarah and I admired what she was doing with her life. Straight out of college she spent a few years toiling away in the corporate world and after she reached a certain financial goal combined with a substantial inheritance, she walked away and started Lift Me Up. The most interesting part of her story was that she witnessed one of her coworkers fall apart as the coworker fought, alongside her child, a devastating illness. That moved Sarah so much she decided to be a part of making a difference in a world that sometimes deals a bad hand from the deck of cards.

After our visit with Sarah concluded, Jacob and I were heading back home in his car listening to some terrible music. It was an uncanny moment when Jacob reached into the glove box, retrieved the silver-rimmed glasses and put them on his face. The universe was reminding me to pay attention. The universe was letting me know that I was exactly where I was supposed to be.

…we need a revolution.

From the expression on my dad's face, he must've deemed he achieved his goal for sending me away for the summer. When I suggested he take us out for dinner, he was shocked at first until I convinced him that I wasn't buttering him up for something tangible. Mainly restoring my cell service was his suspicion, which he did immediately and then he questioned as to whether or not I still wanted to dine out in public. After that, he couldn't comprehend why I was laughing about the whole situation.

While we were eating, I explained my summer experience as best I could. He didn't speak much, but he at least was present and listening intently. His eyes filled with curiosity and with every detail, his head shifted to one side or the other. I was sure he was sitting there wondering who this person was sitting in front him.

Recalling a time that I'd communicated with him so much wasn't in my memory, unless I counted being a chatty five-year-old and back then I'd quit talking to my parents because I was constantly being told to "shut-up". At that age, I had a nanny because my parents were always traveling. My nanny spoke broken English, so I kept most of my conversation between myself, Buzz Lightyear, Woody and occasionally Batman got involved if the crime was too big for the others to solve.

When my parents divorced I felt even more alone so the natural gravitation to other kids my age gave me a platform to express myself and I learned that I could charm the whole playground into paying attention to me, and me only. My action figures were always available, but they didn't interact or give me the attention like I'd wanted; like I needed.

With Jacob and me, our friendship blossomed as a competition for attention, though I'm sure our awareness of what we were competing for was nonexistent. Soon we were best friends and others latched on to our parade.

First was Jayden. We knew Jayden from school, but once we started playing on a football team we spent much more time together and eventually he joined us in one of our sleepovers. Jacob and I would gang up on Jayden in a wrestling match, obviously an early sign of our strong bond.

Second, we befriended Taylor, because she had a childhood crush on Jayden. She was a cheerleader and followed him around after every game, but Jayden never noticed. He only cared about football and getting a higher score on his favorite Play Station game. Later, Taylor moved on to Jacob because she thought the way his hair curled up in back when he sweated was so adorable.

Chloe and Grace might as well have been Taylor's right and left hands and because of that, they became part of the package. With all the girls in tow, we were forced to go roller-skating on occasion, but we went under the agreement that they promise not to complain about whatever action film we chose at the movie theatre.

Austin came along later and he was just always there, like a log that nobody could move. Even when we were young, he was big enough to hide behind, and his cowboy accent caused the other kids to stare at him as if he had a swollen tongue.

As the pack leader, I remember two incidents when I convinced my friends to follow along with what I wanted them to do. On one occasion, after sneaking glimpses from the movie *Helter Skelter* where a cultish maniac led his group in murder and mayhem, I persuaded my classmates to draw swastikas on their foreheads before we went on the playground. It was an innocent maneuver on my part, because my only intent was to frighten the other kids and at the time. I had no idea what that symbol stood for nor did I know anything about Charles Manson. All I knew was, it scared the hell out of me and I thought it would scare the hell out of the others. That was the first time we all got in trouble together. Big trouble. So much, trouble in fact that it took many lengthy conversations for authorities to conclude that I wasn't a sadistic child. Running through a playground pretending to kill children wasn't such a good idea.

Eventually, in the middle of my freshman year I got around to reading the book about the notorious criminal and watching the entire movie on which it was based, and understood the implications of my innocent actions. I related to how manipulating others could be a bad thing if the manipulator took things to the extreme.

Next and a few elementary school years later, I started a trend of using odd colored shoelaces and sporting cartoon character t-shirts. Really, that was Jacob's idea, but I implemented the fad and rejected all the nerds who didn't do the same. I should've known then that Jacob's taste hovered around eccentric. It was interesting to see how quickly white shoelaces caused someone to turn into a goon.

Dad still couldn't believe I didn't want anything other than sharing the news and my revelation. Warning him about what was coming was a must of course and I was surprised when he said he would allow it. Jacob's idea would completely go against the grain of my dad's straight-laced lifestyle.

That night I quietly sat at my desk looking at Caleb's

artwork, a masterpiece in crayon. His parents were kind enough to let me take the work and were so moved that I wanted the treasure that they gave me several pictures of Caleb to go along with it. I needed both as a reminder of where I never wanted to go again, not meaning the camp, but the hell in my own mind. I shared the photos with Jacob and Marissa and in a strange way; Caleb became part of our plan. In remembrance, Caleb served as a motivator to remind us of what we were trying to do.

Since there was a week left before school started, I decided I should probably text Taylor and see if she was back in town. Her reply text read, -still in Cabo until Sun. ttyl @ school. Good times! We needed Taylor for our scheme.

#

Back at camp, Jacob was first to discover that Marissa had moved to our school district and that information helped initiate an idea that could have a lasting impact on our lives and with hope, it might have a lasting imprint on the lives of others.

During the summer, Jacob and I clued Marissa in on the specifics of how our school operated and the dynamics she was about to face. Marissa assured us that she would be fine and that her old school was very similar, only her school was larger with more students in the battle. I had no doubts that Marissa could hold her own in the court of judgment.

#

Homeroom for Taylor, Chloe, and Grace was held in Ms. Broom's room who taught contemporary sociology. The expo board at the front of the room was labeled as such with an enthusiastic "welcome back" added to the end of the class title.

For whatever reason, the school divided homerooms up into genders; girls on one side of the campus and boys on the other. Their attempts to do the same with locker assignments created a fiasco one year, but they had yet to yield to a different homeroom situation, though it had caused several logistical problems.

While waiting for homeroom to begin, Taylor smoothed lotion down the length of her arm trying to keep her tanned skin moisturized. Next to her, Grace stared into a mirror debating whether her new haircut suited the shape of her face while Chloe slurped the last of a diet shake through a straw.

Taylor shoved a bottle of lotion back inside her Prada handbag, "Summer is over. This blows."

"How was Cabo?" Chloe retrieved the straw from the can to save for later.

"Cabo was amazing. Anything is better than this crap!"

"Where was Gavin this morning?" Grace smeared a strip of Carmex across her bottom lip.

"I don't know. He called while I was in Cabo. OMG, guys, somebody totally died while he was at Camp Creepy."

"Camp Creepy. Poor Gavin." Chloe winced.

"Worse than creepy. It happened right in Gavin's cabin." Taylor added.

Earlier that morning in the school parking lot, a long-standing ritual affirmed an ending. Gavin didn't show up in order to wait.

Just as the tardy bell chimed, Marissa entered the classroom and right away, the girls noticed her, the clothes she was wearing, and the shoes on her feet. Along with those observations, they saw someone they had never seen at their school before.

Taylor glared in Marissa's direction, "OMG, another one."

"Are we under a zombie and vampire invasion?" Grace added a swipe to her top lip.

"Right. I saw IT in the parking lot getting out of her car this morning." Chloe said.

There was only one seat remaining in the room and Marissa sat there. Clearly, a seat that other students had avoided because of the location right in front of Taylor and none of them believed it was worth the ridicule they'd endure.

Taylor leaned over her desk, "Honey, it's only August."

Grace chimed in, "Happy Halloween."

Because of the previous warning, Marissa knew who they were and from pictures, what they looked like. Taylor, Grace, and Chloe snickered as Marissa boldly turned to face them without any fear or hesitation. Gavin was correct in assuming Marissa could hold her ground.

"Sweetie, this isn't a scene from The Housewives of Beverly Hills."

Taylor leaned back crossing here arms. "Right. That get up you're wearing is miles away from Rodeo Drive for sure."

Homeroom ended, the girls exited the classroom and huddled by Taylor's locker. Taylor flipped open her cell phone and shut her locker door.

"What's up with that? Two texts and no reply."

Taylor, Grace, and Chloe sneered as Marissa passed by and continued down the hall.

Grace sighed, "Gavin, vanished, abducted by a vampire."

"Well, they've got to feed." Taylor suggested.

#

Proudly, Taylor, Chloe, Grace, Austin, and Jayden honored their earned spot at the senior table. Of course, it wasn't for all seniors — only the popular seniors.

Austin's refurbished accent shined through clearly, "Taylor you look bangin' hot. Summer in Cabo treated you right, girl."

"I'm rocking it." Taylor replied proudly.

"I'm sayin,'" Austin approved.

When I opened the cafeteria door, I heard the chatter ripple in unison. It began at the front of the room and trickled to the rear like a wave from the ocean coming to shore.

"What the…" Jayden was stunned.

"OMG." Taylor, Chloe, and Grace almost stated in unison.

Austin winced, "Oh, now that's just wrong."

I expected the reaction. That morning, Jacob and I were intentionally late for school and steered clear of everyone just for this moment of shock and awe.

In a period of a week, before our schools scheduled start back date, Jacob, Marissa, and I put our plan into action.

We spent a several late nights at a local Bohemian coffee shop on Haywood Street, where I had never been before, scheming, talking, laughing, and mastering a coffee buzz. I learned to love coffee. Who knew I could replace one damaging addiction with another mildly dangerous one? It came as no surprise that Jacob was a regular and all the patrons knew him. Apparently, he'd traded one arena where he was popular for another where eccentric behavior was expected.

The coffee shop's patrons were an eclectic group from all walks of life. On a tiny stage hippies shared poetry, songwriter-singers belted out the blues and, on occasion, radicals spouted off political opinions for whomever was willing to lend an ear. It was rare that anyone listened because the world was sick of the old ideologies that got us to this point in the first place; a clear wreck. Featured mostly was music and I found myself starting to enjoy the bizarre stuff Jacob was listening to constantly. Well, some of it anyway. I could've lived without the boring folk songs, which were similar to country music; the songs all sound so dreadfully woeful but the performers in that place lived and breathed them.

Once we got our plans sorted and over the next few days, Jacob and Marissa transformed me into someone that I only recognized because of the eyes. Makeover in reverse, I felt.

It was an event in itself watching Jacob and Marissa rummage through vintage shops making decisions about what items suited me, the color of my skin, but still had an attention grabbing quality to them. I'd put up an argument about some of the stuff, because some things were too over the top. Mainly, the sky blue shirt with quarter-inch thick white stripe that ran along the thread lines that they were convinced was the dopest shirt in the entire state. I told them, not even if I were dead would I be caught in that shirt.

We spent hours washing, drying, then running over with a car, then again washing and drying a pair of Converse tennis shoes helping them achieve the expended look for the upcoming performance. I'd always wondered to myself how the wearers of those shoes got them to look the way they did. Now, I knew there was an art to finishing the pieces.

The barber thought I was crazy when he held up the mirror for my approval and I couldn't stop laughing. I laughed so hard that tears rolled down my face and I could've sworn that I tore something loose in my stomach. It felt as though I'd done fifty extra push-ups or hauled around a couple of extra pieces of luggage.

Jacob and Marissa laughed as well, but in the confusion, I didn't know if they were laughing at my haircut or laughing at me laughing while I sat crumpled up on the floor suggesting they take me to hospital for an x-ray.

Good ol' Dad knew of the plan and agreed that it was okay, but he didn't jump on board straightaway. As nicely as he could, Dad demanded that I use the back door when I left the house. He politely suggested that the homeowner's association wouldn't approve. When I told Jacob and Marissa about that, I was sure that one of us would end up in the emergency room with a burst appendix. Maybe it was the coffee, but that night I almost peed my pants from laughing so hard.

I finished the final steps to the cafeteria table for my debut.

I positioned my backpack on the senior table, "What's up fellow seniors?"

My senior friends were speechless as they gawped at my multi-colored Mohawk, seventies plaid pants, and my button down cream-colored shirt. It required some acting skill to remain serious while I was looking like a show clown.

Chloe whispered, "Grace you were right."

Grace followed up, "Abducted!"

Jayden's deep voice thundered, "Uh, is the coach

going to allow that?'"

So badly, I wanted to laugh. Jayden was serious, yet what would it really matter since my hair remained hidden underneath the protective gear I wore on my head during a game?

As part of our strategy, Jacob gave me a few minutes to implement shock and awe in the cafeteria and settle in my place amongst the popular kids before he joined the scene.

Jacob heaved the door, passed through and his transformation was as obvious as it was the first day of tenth grade. Currently, he was clean-cut, his hair styled to what society might deem as acceptable hair, wearing what the maker of teenage protocol might consider the right shoes, and he was handsome as ever.

With a drag between each letter Taylor said, "O-M-G!"

Once more, the buzz simmered amongst the students. I never bothered looking behind me because I knew the sight they beheld.

Struggling with the names Austin uttered, "Okay, I give. Wes Craven? M. Night Shyamalan. What movie are we in?"

I dealt my card.

Enthusiastically I expressed, "Senior year," then as serious as Heath Ledger as the Joker from Batman, "Guys we need a revolution!"

Smugly, Taylor put it out there, "Looks like you already had one."

Jayden scoffed, "Doh."

"No, seriously. Let's get outside of the box. Make the last year count." I affirmed while staying in character.

Austin clamored in Tex-speak, "Is that whut you're

tryin' ta do with that? The geeks and nerds have already tried that. It's a not workin' out so good for 'em."

With her mouth still hinged in awe, Taylor added, "Right. Is this a joke? Gavin, tell me this is a joke."

I remained upbeat, "Where is the joke? Let us shake things up a bit!"

Maintaining my composure and a positive attitude, I lifted myself from the table, proceeded to the center of the lunch area and sat down with people that I hadn't spoken to since fourth grade.

Dialing a lid off a Carmex tube, Grace exclaimed, "Rude."

Austin lifted his hand like he was holding a serving platter, "Whut-is-he-doin'?"

Jacob eased through with a lunch tray as if he were waltzing down a catwalk in Milan. Crisp. Cool. Collected. Conforming.

Taylor's eyes widened, "Speaking of banging hot."

"Right!" Chloe stuffed a french-fry in her mouth.

Grace's eyes followed Jacob's movement, "Body snatchers! One turns into a moth and the other a butterfly."

"Girls, don't lose your head," Jayden said.

Harshly, Austin mumbled, "Yeah, that faggot wouldn't let you sit in his ride!"

Rising, Taylor gestured for the girls to follow, "Not that it would matter if he is, but just because he doesn't roll with you butt wads anymore doesn't mean he is gay. Girls?"

Chloe joined Taylor and smirked, "Later, butt wads."

I attempted talking to the kids at the table, but I wasn't getting much out of them. Shock covered their faces both about my new look and the fact that I was giving them any attention at all. Who could blame them; it was so off the wall. I hadn't pre-planned what to say, so "What did you do over the weekend" might be a little forward.

At exactly the same time, Jacob and I peered up at each other and nodded. I surmised that our performance went well. We eyed Marissa and her face was frozen with an anticipatory expression.

What always impressed me about Jacob was his ability to remain cool in any situation. Even before our separation, he was that way. I'd be the first to throw a punch, I never had to, but if it were called for I would've. Jacob would rather talk it out. Perhaps that is why I never had to use a fist; he was there to smooth out any agitation.

For the rest of the afternoon, I ventured about trying to communicate with different students who also weren't very receptive. It was hard to tell if it was the new me or the old me that caused a noticeable cringe when I approached. I felt like a leper or that deranged person who walked around with a swastika tattooed on his forehead.

I was near the end of science hall when Jacob passed by Jayden and Austin. Normally, I would've been standing right there with them, acting like an ass and listening to Austin throw out random remarks directed at students traveling the hall. Austin reached out just at the right time shoving Jacob and causing him to lose his balance. I'd heard about Austin physically assaulting people, but I had never seen it happen right in front of me until today. Feeling prepared to spring into action, I kept my sights in their direction in case I needed to intervene.

"Whoa. Totally unnecessary." Jacob regained his balance.

Jacob continued moving, blowing it off. I knew he was used to the catcalls, but I don't think anyone had ever touched him before.

Jayden thumped Austin on the arm with his fingers. "Dude, what was that for?"

"Three years of nothing, but today he pisses me off."

"Yeah? Well, he isn't some wimp like these other swimmers!" Jayden warned.

Reading his expression, Austin didn't like what Jayden was implying. Though Austin was pretty much a tree, most of his bulk was fat, unlike Jacob who was just as tall with muscles from head to toe. Obviously, Austin had forgotten that Jacob was a football player before. How Jacob maintained his fitness after he quit the team was his own secret.

When Taylor slipped by I had to grab her by the arm; she didn't recognize me in my new garb.

"I was really close to slugging you."

"Funny."

"Gavin, that hair. You look like an idiot."

"It's not that bad."

"You don't even sound like yourself."

"I don't sound like myself?"

"No. What are you doing?"

"Taylor, I need your help."

"I knew it. You did drugs this summer and you're an addict."

"Taylor come on."

"Come on what?"

"The game. Let's take it up a notch."

"The game Gavin? Seriously?"

"Okay, we'll call it an experiment."

...taking it up a notch.

Patronizing the coffee shop on Haywood, I chugged my coffee while Marissa and I waited for Jacob to arrive. Oddly, when he first strolled through the entry, he looked funny to me, not like himself and I deduced I'd grown accustomed to attire with a bit more flare.

Smiling, Jacob slid out the chair and sat down. "Troublemakers!" he laughed.

"Okay, so how'd I do?"

"You'll definitely get a nomination for your outstanding performance as a loser."

"If you two could have seen how people were looking at you. Watching all that play out. Having the inside scoop about what was going on was very interesting." Marissa said.

I pushed away from the table, "Going for a refill. Jacob you want something? Marissa?"

"Coffee, no magical additives."

Marissa held out her fingers while shaking them, "Anxiety, no thanks. I'm good."

"Be right back."

"Wow, his attitude is 360," she said to Jacob.

"Actually, that's the real him. Haven't seen that in a long time; haunting really."

"So, how did he get so jaded?"

"Spending all that time trying to impress people will make anyone crazy. Just compare it to the celebrities who lose their heads."

I returned to the table and for the first time in a long time, I felt, what's the word? Happy. It almost sounded foreign.

"I feel liberated!"

Marissa suggested, "It's the coffee."

"So, what do we do now?" I took a swig from the mug.

"You just keep doing you," Jacob replied. "You're the only one who can pull it off. There's no way that I can go back. Just taking off the clown nose wouldn't be enough."

Marissa tilted forward, "Do you think doing this is really going to prove or accomplish anything?"

Jacob shrugged his shoulders, "Maybe nothing. Maybe something. It's just an experiment in human behavior. No harm."

"I talked to Taylor. I think she is on board with the plan. Maybe. Hard to read from our conversation."

"Gavin, she has followed you around for years. She'll do it."

"And for now we keep quiet about us?"

"For now. You made sure she understood that you were serious?"

"I don't know if she thinks I'm serious, but I know she thinks I'm an addict."

Laughing, Marissa pointed to the coffee mug, "You are."

I wasn't quite convinced our quest would work either.

When the storm calmed back at Camp Lift Me Up and we could carry on a conversation without disruptions and tantrums, Jacob relayed his idea via a skilled presentation.

The ultimate goal of his scheme was to see if I had the ability to sway the entire school to ride the train of my extreme alteration. Jacob was convinced that just like the shoestrings and Cookie Monster t-shirts that everyone would transform to a goblin, but only if a few of the popular kids got on board.

#

Across town in Taylor's bedroom she curiously stared into a mirror flipping her long blond hair from one side to the other. Grace and Chloe rested on the bed singing along with the radio tunes while experimenting with different colors of nail polish.

Taylor rotated around in the chair, "Maybe Gavin is right. We should shake things up. I mean, why not?"

Chloe wiped a color off a fingernail, "OMG, what are you saying?"

Grace blew on her hand as she moved from the bed, "I think you should kick Gavin to the curb, who has apparently lost his mind, and go after Jacob."

"Well, he has obviously come out of the dreadful coma he was in. You know, I could change a little here and there in case Jacob is into the way those dark water swimmers looks."

Chloe carefully brushed a fingernail, "Speaking of swimmers, where did that sheisty girl come from?"

"Who cares really?" Grace blew an opposite hand.

Taylor shifted her hair again, "I don't, that's for sure."

Chloe tightened the lid of a polish bottle, "What are you going to do about Gavin?"

"We're not married. Besides, I don't want to hook up with someone who looks like they came from the scary side of London."

Grace perked up, "And Jacob is the prime of prime. Well, now that he has recovered, obviously."

"Right." Taylor said then bite her lip.

Taylor's phone signaled an incoming text. Picking up the phone, she moved and sat on the bed beside Chloe.

Taylor shuffled open the phone, "Speaking of the clown."

She viewed a text from Gavin, which read –R U down? Taylor quickly thumbed a reply message –I'm down.

"So, are you guys up for a challenge?" Taylor questioned with a hint of sneakiness in her eyes.

"As in?" Chloe perked up with the invitation.

Fooling with her hair, Taylor rose from the bed, "Taking it up a notch?"

Taylor, Grace, and Chloe began putting together their own treasure map for change. They needed to go shopping of course, and Taylor comically demanded that Chloe highlight dark eyeliner twice on their list of "must haves". The girls spent a half hour trying to decide what magazines to turn to for inspiration. Chloe suggested Field & Stream, not knowing exactly what kind of publication it was. Later, they referenced the television show, LA INK for ideas.

Finally, amid much debate, they settled on queuing movies at Netflix, numerous vampire themes and a documentary titled, "Shockumentary" and its cousin, "Party Monster". Not that any of them were big readers, but once they finished watching, "Party Monster", they ended up reading the book from which the movie was adapted, penned by James St. James — a comical recollection that was originally known as "Disco Bloodbath". They found that though the story revealed some disturbing aspects, it was a funny read overall. Taylor commented that she and James viewed the world with the same humorous candor. Following the read, she wanted to meet him, believing he might have some advice on how to look monstrous, yet fabulous. Preferably, advice that wouldn't involve Special K or black tar heroin.

The race to discover a new look had begun.

…it's not Saks.

From Grace's suggestion, Taylor had one thing on her mind the following day and that was to lure Jacob into her web. If Gavin wanted to play dress-up and mingle with those treading water, it was fine with her. Taylor could move on and find someone else. Or she could move on to someone from the past. Since Jacob had approval from the social order, he became the target of Taylor's flirtation. If she landed Jacob, the appeal of playing dress up with Gavin would've been discarded as quickly as used kitty litter.

It was assumption in the halls of learning that, Taylor and Gavin were a couple. They had dated, but it wasn't long until they both settled in the fact they were better suited as friends. Their scant moments of intimacy clarified to them that something was missing.

For the longest time, Taylor clung to a belief that someday Gavin would change his mind, turn around, declare his love for her and they would eventually live that life people call happily ever after. Gavin held none of those same feelings.

Prior to Taylor and Gavin having a go at a relationship, Taylor's jealousy over Gavin and Jacob's tight bond made the allure of capturing Jacob even more tempting. What might be a better way to lure back the object of her affection than fraternizing with his former best friend, she thought? Besides, Jacob was hot.

Watching from afar, Austin witnessed Taylor slinking over to Jacob as he organized the books in his locker. Jacob hadn't noticed her lurking nearby until he closed the locker and she crept in behind the door.

Taylor grinned mischievously, "Looks like summer

treated you well."

"Watch out Taylor, if the mafia sees you talking with the enemy, your standing in the social order might be in question."

"Jacob, I am the social order."

"Right. How quickly I've forgotten. If memory serves me at all, I vaguely remember you were one of the ones who cast me back to sea with the other swimmers."

"Well, Jacob you've got to admit that over one summer you morphed into someone who had obviously spent one too many nights on a haunted tour of Savannah, Georgia."

Jacob looked upward, eyes directed to the ceiling, "Ah. So, if I were in a car wreck and mangled, I would somehow be a lesser person because of my scars?"

"That's not exactly fair."

Jacob shifted and began walking while speaking over his shoulder.

"Not fair. Clearly the point. Sleep on it."

#

Classes bored Taylor in a different way than they bored the typical student. Her aptitude for remembering information from one reading meant that she didn't have to pay attention. Taylor's long-standing placement on the academic honor rolls was proof of her excelled learning. She was far better suited for college where she could have the option to show up for class or not, so long as she passed the exams and submitted any required essays and such.

She endured her own pressures at home since she hailed from a long line of old money — Ivy League educated parents and stuffy family ritualistic formalities. Taylor considered herself more modern and scoffed at long-standing traditions.

Taylor withheld cringing when Austin parked his hefty butt in the desk in front of her. In a group setting, she mastered tolerating his presence, but one on one, not so much. At least it gave her something to do, ridicule and intimidate.

"Hey Taylor, what's up with the scrub?"

Taylor rolled her eyes, "Up in my business?"

"Well, you know, just looking out for my girl."

"My girl? You had better stick to the kiddy pool, Tex. Your arm floats couldn't hold you up in this pond."

Dumbfounded, Austin slumped forward, "Why does it gotta be like that?"

Taylor leaned closer, "If you haven't figured me out by now you never will. Odds are the latter. Your game doesn't work in this rodeo. You see, I know the game. I invented it. The only thread of hope for you, and believe me it was a thin thread, was Gavin. So don't think you can wade in a big sea with this big fish."

Austin snarled, "Is that right? What got you on a bitch pony?"

"The saddle I ride takes me where I want to go, to get what I want to get. Real leather, no uh, pleather. Right now, since your boy has been bitten on the neck and slid head first into a dark comic book tale, I've got my eyes focused on the sunset."

"You know what I think?" Austin questioned.

"Really? No, but do share. I've got forty minutes to exploit before the bell rings."

Austin's accent curled to the top, "Global warmin' has deep fried all of you. Knew you were tightly wound, but I think you got too close to the equator this summer; tightened you up a notch. Who needs ya!"

Taylor shut it down, "Wow, I'm impressed. You know the word equator. Anyway, now, that we've narrowed down the list of prom possibilities we can all sleep soundly."

Austin sat speechless. Class began and ended without any further exchanges, but Austin stored the scene in a running loop within his internal vision.

Later in the hall as Austin switched books at his locker, Taylor breezed by tossing a folded up piece of paper to Austin. Austin's hands jerked and fumbled trying to catch the floating sheet. Printed on the flyer was an advertisement inviting upper classmen to reserve space for the upcoming annual prom.

Walking away, Taylor sinisterly smirked, "Some bag ladies at the other end of the hall, might find a candidate!"

Angrily, Austin wadded the prom flyer into a ball, hurled it through the air like a baseball, and hit a passing student directly in the head.

Taylor giggled about Austin all the way to the media center. Once she was inside, she placed her books and purse on a long, narrow table. Her silly mood snuffed out when she caught sight of Jacob and Marissa flipping through a magazine, laughing, appearing as if they had known each other forever.

Hiding in between two rows of book shelving, Taylor pressed digits on a cell phone.

"Grace, what kind car was that creepy new girl driving?"

#

Nearing the end of the school day, Taylor tactfully persuaded a teacher to excuse her from class early by telling her she had terrible cramps and must see the school nurse because the pain was so bad that she didn't think she could drive home.

Following that up, Taylor brilliantly performed for the nurse. Taylor assured her that if she wasn't able to get home soon and take her medication they would need to call an ambulance to transport her off school grounds. Every couple of seconds Taylor curled over in agonizing pain to magnify her dramatic plea.

Reluctantly, and after getting permission from Taylor's parents, the nurse penned the necessary checkout form. Shortly after, Taylor rushed toward the parking lot. From Grace's description, it didn't take her any time to locate Marissa's car.

#

Marissa said goodbye to Jacob and headed for her locker for a book swap. When she swung open the metal door, a prominently placed picture of Caleb centered the rear wall adjacent to a photograph of her father that she had hung there on the first day of school.

For several days, Marissa's anxiety level had been high, but making it through a couple of days enabled her to relax a bit. Like she'd mentioned to Gavin and Jacob, this school was much smaller and she believed there were more people aligning with where she stood in the social hierarchy of high school life.

Among other obvious reasons, the fact that most of the student body at her other school had parents rolling in cash was a crucial factor in Marissa's mother's decision to relocate them to a smaller suburban area. Getting away from a constant reminder of what they had lost was best.

Having a couple of new friends in Gavin and Jacob helped relieve some of the angst that death, moving, and a school change would cause.

It was clear by her jovial demeanor as she pranced

through the courtyard that she was the happiest she had been since the passing of her father.

Marissa's mind was focused elsewhere as she got in the car and closed the door, so she hadn't noticed anything different. After firing the engine, and looking to the rear, Marissa reversed the vehicle then turned to face the front of the car. In bright red lipstick written across the windshield were bold letters that spelled out, BLACK WIDOW.

With anticipation, Taylor lingered near the flagpole peeking toward the direction of Marissa's car. She spied as if she had placed a bomb on the undercarriage and any second now with the flip of the starter-switch the car would explode into a fiery ball of flame.

A blissful mood swiftly exchanged for a sour one while Marissa hastily forced the car gears into drive, slammed her foot down on the accelerator, which raced the car forward like the space shuttle shooting from a platform at Cape Canaveral.

When the car jetted by the flagpole, Taylor resumed curling over, only this time it was real and the pain was from laughter.

"Maniac black widow, even."

#

With the exception of the custodial staff and a few players that linger after football practice, Austin being one of them, the school grounds were mostly deserted. Since fall was in full swing it was already getting dark, which gave the impression that it was a lot later than it really was.

"Hello," Austin paused, "They're done with my car, and you have to take me to the garage. Just pick me up in front of the school."

Before Austin left for Texas for the summer, he'd

dropped his car off at an auto repair shop so a mechanic could replace the engine. Due to a certain part being on backorder there was a repair delay and the car wasn't ready by the time he returned from visiting his grandmother, so he was stuck waiting for a ride.

Austin performed a solo two-step on the cement stairs in front of the school when across the lawn he caught a glimpse of Gavin struggling with a backpack and a large load of sports equipment. From out of nowhere, just as Gavin reached Jacob's car, Jacob trotted up beside him.

"Hey there buddy, need some help?"

"Can you believe I have to carry all this shit for the show?

By show, Gavin referenced to the fact that he disliked football more and more, but he continued participating and felt obligated since he had been part of the team for so long.

Jacob grabbed some equipment form Gavin, "Everything is a theatrical event."

"Right!"

Like a spy, Austin sunk back behind a stacked brick column watching Gavin and Jacob. Jacob opened the trunk of the Volkswagen, which happened to be in the front, another trait of that particular vehicle, and he and Gavin loaded the gear inside. As Jacob and Gavin packed the trunk, they were smiling and joking around.

Observing the two old friends together left Austin confused. Making it even odder, Austin witnessed Gavin placing his arms straight down at his side and facing Gavin, Jacob moved closer wrapping his arms around him in a bear hug. Then clamping them together he lifted Gavin off the pavement.

Austin raised his brow, "Table gum. Pink table gum,"

his voice jagged, "I'll be damned. Cowboys riding off into the sunset. Cock-a-doodle-doo."

#

If someone had told me before the summer began that the following fall Jacob would pick me up after practice and we would be riding down the road in a restored car listening to techno music, I wouldn't have believed them. It was happening and I still didn't believe it.

Although extremely reluctant at first, I'd begun encouraging Jacob to introduce me to more of the different music he'd become familiar with. Along with that, the appeal of earth shattering clothing had grown more interesting. It was as though I had been given an opportunity to serve as an art gallery in motion. The designer labels demanded attention, but now I wasn't a moving billboard with a huge brand name strapped across my chest. It never occurred to me to sell oneself and not assist in increasing the market value of someone else's product. Really, on some level it was absurd to do so. Do people even realize they are a walking commercial?

Jacob lowered the volume on the radio, "She was very coy, but I knew she would come on to me and just like I said, I gave her something to think about, but you know Taylor. Who knows if it registered with her at all?"

"So did you call her?"

"Yes, she agreed to meet me later."

"Well, good luck with that. What are you going to do when she wants to wrap her finger around your brown curls?" I kidded.

"Shut up."

Since Taylor had influences of her own, we had to get her involved in our plot. Jacob and I both recognized that underneath the Mac makeup and flowing blond mane that she wasn't as cold-hearted as she came across. Discussing the matter, I suggested to Jacob that maybe she suffered the same as I did on the inside; that we had both gotten trapped in a never-ending game of egocentricity. I might've been to blame for her callousness that resulted from a dream she held that someday we would be more than friends. In a sense, we fed off each other in a distinctive co-dependent nature.

Arriving at my house, I exited Jacob's car and sat down on the drive. He pulled away and headed to the coffee shop where he would meet up with Taylor.

It was still surreal that we had reunited.

#

Showing up at the Bohemian hotspot was a bold move for Taylor. It wasn't common for the country club crowd to associate with the caffeinated clientele. Her parents wouldn't be thrilled either if gossip made the rounds that their daughter was seen in a certain part of town.

Taylor showed up as Jacob was lifting two mugs off the service counter, so he motioned for her to take a vacant table near a large window facing Haywood Street.

Looking uncomfortable Taylor lifted her mug, "Thanks for inviting me."

"Sure. Thought I owed you an apology for being such a douche earlier today."

Taylor eyes scanned the room, "No worries. So, this is where you've been hiding?"

"My favorite place. It's so real don't you think?" Jacob sipped from a mug.

"Interesting."

From the position where Taylor was sitting, Jacob was the only one able to see Marissa when she crossed through the front door, walked over, and placed an order with the barista.

"Taylor, I know this isn't your kind of thing, but good for you for giving it a chance."

Marissa seated herself at a nearby table out of Taylor's sight, but within Jacob's view. Initially, Gavin was going to come along too, but at the last minute, the group decided it was too early to let Taylor in on the specifics; mainly their unification and doing so might hinder their objectives.

Once Jacob and Marissa finally confessed their crushes on each other, Marissa couldn't stand the thought of Jacob being there alone with that "bimbo" which was how Marissa referred to Taylor. Since Taylor could only stay for thirty minutes, Marissa wanted to witness her squirm in discomfort. She was convinced that Taylor wouldn't touch anything, fearing she would chip a fingernail. Much to Marissa's surprise, Taylor was actually drinking the coffee.

Outside on Haywood Street, Austin's newly repaired vehicle crept to a crawl in front of the coffee shop. Austin eased down the window for a clearer view of Jacob and Taylor. Both of his hands tightly clenched the steering wheel as the car picked up speed.

Earlier when Austin retrieved his car from the auto shop, he couldn't wait to scurry over to Taylor's house, rap on the front door and clue Taylor in about what he had seen at school. When Austin arrived on the street just near Taylor's house, she was backing out of the drive so he trailed her to the coffee shop.

Austin was confident that with both Gavin and Jacob out of the picture he might have a solid shot with Taylor and her banging body. By the time he caught up with her on Haywood, Taylor was gliding through the entrance door of the coffee shop. Anxious to tell the news, Austin cruised back and forth on Haywood like a celebrity stalker.

Meanwhile, inside, the whole time Jacob and Taylor were talking; Marissa sat within Jacob's sight satirizing every move that Taylor made. Taylor never noticing that a couple of times Jacob fought back laughs because of Marissa's exaggerated movements. Not stopping with Taylor, Marissa copied Jacob's notable hair flip as well.

Finally, after twenty minutes, Austin gave up lurking because of his curfew and set out for home. Ten minutes after that, Taylor's allotted time was up and she headed for home herself.

Jacob pulled his car to the curb next to Marissa who waited just in front of the coffee shop and she got inside.

Shaking his index finger, "You are too much."

"That was the most disgusting thing I've ever seen." Marissa exclaimed.

#

Chloe and Grace were waiting in Taylor's room by the time she returned home. True to actor's form, Taylor had convinced her parents that she and the girls had to have a mid-week study session for some ridiculously complicated math quiz.

She grinned as she entered her room and immediately Chloe blurted out in celebration.

"OMG, you hooked the fish."

"Was there any doubt? Taylor plopped down on the bed.

The real reason Chloe and Grace came over had nothing at all to do with homework. While Taylor was off casting a line, Chloe and Grace had gone shopping.

"So, what did you guys get?" Taylor sat up.

Grace began pulling articles of clothing from a thrift store bag.

Taylor's jaw dropped, "OMG, you've got to be kidding.

Holding a candy bar like a pointer Chloe stated, "It's not Saks."

Originally the girls had planned going shopping together, but when the invitation call came from Jacob, Taylor suggested that the other two stick with the trip so they could get started with their new look.

#

Jacob reached for the radio, "Are you going to be able to handle this?"

As Jacob's car halted near Marissa's parked car, she pondered his question as she reached for the door handle.

"As long as you don't look like you're so into it."

"It's just a role."

Marissa pushed the door open, "Uggh."

Jacob was flattered by the jealousy, but couldn't resist expressions caused by the humor he found in Marissa's uggh.

…ear piercing scream.

Most of the time, my dreams were wildly amusing, consisting of some silly configuration of what happened during the day or days before. Guilt was haunting me as I dreamt about Caleb.

Outside of myself, I noticed my body soundly sleeping in my bedroom. There was no knock and my bedroom door crept open, a dim light seeped through the crack as the space between the door and the jamb grew wider. Wearing pajamas, Caleb glided across the floor, almost sneaking, until he reached my bedside. As he leaned inward to where I was sleeping, I notice his brightly colored PFD. He cupped his thin hand and inched closer to the side of my head then he whispered.

"I have to go to the bathroom."

I saw myself startled.

"What the…"

Suddenly, as a witness to my dream, I watched as marshmallows rained down from the sky like hail pounding my body into submission until I drew up into a fetal position.

When I came to, I hurled out of the bed fighting the air with my hands. Realizing it was a dream I couldn't help but suffer both sadness and anger. I crawled back into bed and began pounding my fist into the mattress as tears collected on the pillowcase.

\#

By the time lunch period arrived and much like a day back at camp when I was exhausted from lack of sleep, I needed a nap. I'm not sure what time my haunting dream woke me up, but for the rest of the night I didn't sleep very much. I couldn't get Caleb off my mind. Much like before,

I think by the time I began falling back to sleep the sun was rising.

I seized my position of the day in the lunch area right in the center of the room so I could catch the full effect of the room's reaction from what was about to go down.

When the cafeteria door opened, I had to fight back an overwhelming desire to jump up and shout hooray. One habit I hadn't stamped out of my behavior was my self-inflicted need to remain cool and collected.

Typical Taylor showed up shortly after the other students had settled down with their mashed potatoes, but this time Grace and Chloe were stuck to her sides like the right and left holsters of a gun belt. Not surprising, the roar and gasp increased the noise level a notch.

Chloe and Grace's hair looked like cotton candy. Cotton candy caught in a rainstorm. The pinkish purple locks set off the color pallet of plaid shirts, corduroy miniskirts, and black fingerless gloves. The horizontally striped knee-high socks were perfectly grounded with gray Doc Martin's that covered their feet. Their faces took the look to another level and it appeared as though they had intentionally shoved them into the powder and water mixture the staff called gravy. Even the scariest clowns couldn't compete.

Looking terrified, mostly out of place, Grace and Chloe found some random table to join and them doing so made me want to burst into a rolling fit of laughter combined by a boisterous Marine hoorah.

Causing Marissa to cringe, Taylor joined Jacob where he had been sitting for a little over two years now.

Praising Taylor, Jacob said, "Nice Look!"

"Then why is everyone staring?" Taylor did a once-over on the sea of diners.

Jacob mused, "Taylor, they stared at you before. It didn't bother you then. Just ignore it. That's what I did."

Taylor hanging her head low, who'd a thought it? Definitely not I, yet I had no sympathy for her because she needed that, that moment, as did I for myself at one point.

I found it interesting that we noticed people staring when in actuality they'd been staring at us all along. The staring was for different reasons, but either way the object of the stare was still under examination.

#

Marissa spent most of her free time in the media center reading. For her, reading allowed her a means of escaping a world she viewed as a strange place with unrealistic expectations of human nature. She enjoyed poring over autobiographies written by those who had survived their own struggles in the quest to find meaning in the universe. Her personal mission sought affirmation that her internal struggle wasn't something that she might've imagined into being.

Whatever Austin and Jayden were doing in there was anyone's guess; most likely one of the two had followed a girl into the media center or they'd taken the liberty of visiting because a teacher had assigned a project, granting them permission to do so. The odds were more in favor of the first choice.

Since they were killing time or whatever they were there for, Marissa couldn't help but overhear the discussion because the two were sitting right behind her. Ignoring Austin's drawl and Jayden's masculine voice wasn't easy to do. Aiding in the attention grabbing was their boisterous lack of maturity coming across in the conversation as they named names.

"Dude, I'm serious." Austin tapped his fingers on the

tabletop.

Jayden turned stern, "Not Gavin. You're delirious."

Austin slouched, "Maybe they've been hiding all along."

"No way."

Austin sat up and leaned onto the table, "Think about it. They were best friends and then all of sudden they weren't."

Jayden shrugged, "Bogus."

"Dude, it was a long hug! A long, long hug."

Marissa gathered up her books, glaring at Austin and Jayden as she left the media center. Marissa's thoughts shifted into high gear, pondering someone's speculation, which related to miniscule observations she contemplated back at Camp Lift Me Up.

#

Inside the bathroom, all of the stall doors were hinged open except for one. Washing her hands while looking at the mirror, Marissa noticed that her eyes were bloodshot from reading too long.

Causing her to grimace, someone rigorously gagging inside the closed stall echoed off the white tiled walls. A few more chokes later and the splat of liquid hitting water brought Marissa to a brief heave herself. Luckily, the purging ceased, the toilet flushed, saving Marissa from hurling.

A latch clicked, the laminate door screeched open and Taylor exited wiping off her mouth with a neatly folded mound of toilet paper.

Without any embarrassment, Taylor rested her purse down on the floor, reached out and with the top of her hand forced the handle controlling the water flow upward so she could rinse her mouth.

Taylor was attentive that Marissa was staring at her in disgust and it was very clear to Marissa what she was doing inside the stall, because Taylor didn't look sick at all.

Taylor shifted her head to one side, "We've all got problems sweetie."

Like a debutant, Taylor left the restroom without Marissa speaking a word in response. Nevertheless, what could Marissa say since she was floored by the fact that the "bimbo" was purging.

#

One of the only classes Taylor, Austin, Jacob, Marissa, and I had at the same time was Ms. Broom's contemporary sociology. A last required course for graduation.

"Everyone in their assigned seats?" Ms. Broom situated herself behind a podium.

It never failed that some students needed to switch seats; somehow, they assumed the day would eventually arrive when Ms. Broom might refrain from checking the roll.

"Last session we were beginning to discuss acceptable reasons for war. Any thoughts? Jacob?"

"Never."

Ms. Broom removed her glasses, "What about the World Trade Center towers?"

Jacob answered, "The attackers are dead."

Very seriously, Ms. Broom questioned, "True. Then the United States went to war with whom?"

"We started a war that I'm not so sure had anything to do with the towers truthfully."

This was a serious conversation that divided many groups across the land of the free and around the world, but I understood where Jacob was coming from.

Jacob continued, "Besides, if it did have something to

do with what happened in New York, what has been solved? We are still in the Middle East among other places, and this supposed enemy is still out there waiting in the wings and now, personally, I feel that misguided action has fueled an already volatile fire. We're still at Ground Zero."

I noticed Austin drape over the front of his desk, which obviously represented his feelings on the subject.

Austin spoke out of turn, "Dude, they want to kill us!"

"Now we have two groups wanting to kill each other?" Jacob responded in the way Jacob could, thought provoking.

Ms. Broom moved forward, "Gavin, your thoughts?"

"I'd agree with Jacob…"

Before I had the chance to add my theories, Austin's mouth snapped uncontrollably.

"You would!" Austin sounded repulsed.

"Austin," Ms. Broom scolded, "Gavin, finish."

"Military actions should be defensive only. The United States spends far too much time and money getting involved in issues all over the world. My point is why should America police the world? From a financial standpoint, don't our cities have problems of their own that need attention? Wouldn't the effect be greater if our borders and points of entry into the country were more secure? I mean, imagine the amount of money spent funding the war in Iraq. Now, imagine that money spent building schools, houses or providing clean water or food for people, all people here and abroad who go without. But we do both. We bomb. We rebuild. Perhaps we should cut to chase and start with the rebuilding. Which builds peace maybe?"

Ms. Broom pondered, "Sounds logical."

"Sounds nuts!" Austin blurted.

"Well then Austin what is your opinion?" Ms. Broom returned to the podium.

"The U.S. should wipe 'em all out. Every single place that causes a problem then we wouldn't have problems anymore."

Ms. Broom scoffed, "Sounds nuts."

Laughter covered the span of the room as Jacob raised his hand.

"Yes Jacob?"

"It's the media generating fear and brainwashing people and that allows politicians to get away with what they're doing and sadly it affects the mentality of some people."

Jacob motioned toward Austin and the students broke into laughter once again and so did I. Sitting there listening to Austin ramble, I began to see him in a completely new light.

#

The standoff continued during our afternoon practice on the football field. It was apparent during every play we ran that Austin was more aggressive, the aggression mainly aimed at me and I experienced the pain every time he tried to plow me into the earth. Jayden noticed as well and spoke up about Austin's behavior.

"Dude, lighten up!"

Austin never answered but as we lined up for another play, I saw him staring right at me grinding his teeth into his mouthpiece. I didn't get it. Was Austin pissed off at me because I had an opinion or because I agreed with Jacob and not the ideology of the insane?

It became clear that he was after me. The coach had blown the whistle at least five times, but Austin kept me pinned to the ground. Our fellow teammates broke it up and heaved the two of us off the turf. Charging like an ox, Austin surged toward me and I thrust out my arms to hold him off.

"What the hell is your problem?" I bellowed.

Austin continued pressing forward, spit seeping through his mouthpiece as he got his face right up in mine.

"I know about you, sunshine."

"Get off me!" I said as I managed to shove Mr. Potato Head backward.

Austin ripped his helmet from his head, "All this time you had us fooled!"

Confused I responded, "What are you talking about?"

Did he know that the vamped up exterior was hiding the person trapped in a dark corner screaming, "Let me out"? No, that couldn't be the answer. Austin was not that bright. I was judging, yes, but surely, Austin's wooden mind wasn't capable of calculating the psychological inner workings of mine.

#

Jacob and I sped down the highway in his flashy car as I air drummed along with the percussion solo of some Swedish band when his phone rang.

"Hey Taylor are you going to make it?"

"Oh Jacob I can't. Got to do time with the oldies. I lost weight; I think they think I'm on drugs. So cliché."

"Sorry about that. So, I will talk to you later." Jacob completed the call.

My drum solo ended, "She isn't coming?"

"The Country Clubbers want her head."

Jacob had invited Taylor to join us at the coffee house where we would finally formally introduce Marissa and then she would discover that Jacob and I were solid friends again. By now, we believed it was safe to explain to Taylor what we were secretly up to. I crossed my fingers hoping that she would take it well.

Much to my surprise, Jacob was right so far. I had noticed a slow progression of change in our school. Nothing major, but here and there my awareness acknowledged that students were stepping up their game. Well, our game. The way people dressed was different and few social circles were integrating. How we would close the game exactly was still up in the air, but ultimately we wished to express our ideas about cliques, clichés, and stereotypes. With any luck, masses of people might come to terms with something I had recognized, that we all want the same thing. Understanding. Acceptance. Love. What we needed to learn was that the obstacles we place in our path are merely self-created hurdles.

"Austin was acting like a complete a-hole."

"Why?"

"I guess he was pissed off that I didn't agree with him in class."

"Did anybody agree with him?"

"I've never put much thought into the ramblings of a mad ox."

"I told you a long time ago that he was a tool."

That was about the extent of Jacob's response when I told him about Austin's behavior on the field. It was true that he had expressed to me back in ninth grade that he didn't think that Austin had his head on straight. Jacob went on to say to me that he had heard that Texas, as a whole, thinks it is its own country. Whatever the case, I didn't think Texas had much to do with Austin's behavior.

By the time we arrived at the coffee shop, Marissa was already sitting inside listening to a self-proclaimed communist reciting poetry about the human condition.

"Hey guys."

We both said in unison, "S'up?"

"Where's the Prom Queen?"

Jacob answered, "Said her parents wanted to talk. They think she's doping. Weight loss or something."

Marissa hesitated, "Hum, well, I'm pretty sure I know what that is all about."

Curious I asked, "What do you mean?"

"It's not dope."

Intrigued, Jacob tuned in, "What do you know?"

"Purging."

To which I said, "Gross."

"What makes you think she is purging?" Jacob wondered.

"Girl's bathroom. I walked in on her."

"Not to sound cruel, but I'm not surprised." Jacob said.

"Well, like she said to me. We all got problems, sweetie."

I lifted my coffee mug, "I'll toast to that."

"Guys, I hate to, but I've got to go. My mother seemed lonely when I left."

I added, "Me too. My dad is going to be raising hell with me anyway. He'll never buy it that practice ran late. I guess since Taylor didn't come we didn't accomplish anything."

Jacob pleaded, "Can't we hang for just a little while longer? I want to hear this next guy. Brilliant sound."

"I feel so bad for my mom, Jacob, I can't. Gavin, if you need a lift I can drop you off." Marissa suggested.

"Dude I'd stay, but he'll turn off my phone and God knows what else. Jacob, you'll be okay here by yourself?"

"Gavin, you know how I roll. I handled it last year

when I was by myself. I'm a big boy."

With that statement, I felt a fleeting tinge of guilt and not knowing what else to do, I gave Jacob a long hug goodbye. I guessed it was a silent apology for the one I hadn't gotten around to giving him yet.

Marissa was probably ready to get me out of her car after I'd practically climbed the walls, ceiling and left indentations in the dashboard while finger drumming to the rhythm of my newest favorite song.

Reeling with a caffeine buzz, I left the car and danced in the front of my house as Marissa peeled away.

When I got inside, the distraction served well because my dad said nothing about homework as he lectured and I heard homeowner's association quite a few times. In my high, dad could've suspected illegal drugs, but he didn't, since I was already subject to random testing for substance abuse. No locks, no social networks, and no drugs. No stimulating the autocratic homeowner's association.

#

Through applause, Jacob revealed his appreciation for the crooner he had waited around to hear which concluded his night. Unlike the other Bohemians in the crowd, he had school the next day.

Jacob, geared high from the caffeine too, merrily shuffled from side to side on the sidewalk heading to the nearby lot to his car.

Reaching the lot, Jacob slid one hand into his pant pocket fishing around for car keys. In one unexpected swift motion, he was jumped from behind. The sudden jolt knocked the wind out of him and he struggled to catch his breath as he slammed forward to the ground. The attacker still latched on to Jacob's back, followed his body down to the pavement, and immediately began whaling on his back with two-closed fists. As the person continued the assault, a cell phone shot across the pavement and a wallet dropped down to the asphalt. The aggressor jumped to his feet and began forcefully kicking Jacob in the head when out of the dark a female produced an ear-piercing scream.

"Stop it," followed with a scream, "Stop it!"

If it hadn't been for the passerby, the beating might've continued. The criminal quickly fled on foot as the frantic woman fumbled with a phone desperately trying to dial 911.

Underneath a dimly lit streetlight, Jacob's body crumpled, torn and beaten, rested lifeless on the cold jagged pavement. His clear olive color complexion was hidden behind gashes and smeared blood. Fragments of dirt, sand and pea-sized pebbles clung to the thick red fluid seeping from the gaping wounds. Sediment was ground into Jacob's forehead from the force of the kicking. His bottom lip, split down the center, revealed three teeth barely clinging to his gum. His hair was matted together and plastered along both sides his face.

Emergency vehicles arrived with lights flashing, sirens echoing through the night and paramedics swung into action. Urgently, Police officers stretched police tape around poles and around the rear of Jacob's car, where splattered blood covered the driver's side door.

As a crowd gathered at the edge of the lot, officers noted whatever information the singular eyewitness could offer in her emotionally distraught state. The metal gurney rattled as the technician hoisted it out of the ambulance.

Delicately, they lifted Jacob's body from the ground as the flashing lights reflected the shimmer of the glossy red blood covering their protective white gloves. Following a muffled grunt, a cough coiled blood from Jacob's mouth as his head fell to the side.

…could've died right then.

Not a single dream haunted me, as did the night before and once I finally achieved sleep after floating for hours on the top layer of a caffeine high, I slept soundly.

Morning came and my new addiction drew me in the direction of a coffee maker before I'd taken my first leak of the day.

"Morning Dad."

"Morning. Starting to enjoy coffee, I see."

Like a fiend, I answered, "Absolutely!"

Though I'd slept fine, I was running late for school. Rushing to get dressed, I phoned Jacob several times to give him the heads up that it might take me a few minutes to meet him on the driveway. There was no answer but that was normal because he was probably zooming along a street somewhere wrapped up in a techno-electronic rhapsody and his cell phone's ring-tone was blending in perfectly with the tune or the distinctive sound of the vehicle's engine.

"Gavin, aren't you usually gone by now?"

For a second I wanted to take the opportunity and suggest that if I owned a car I would've left minutes ago, however I held my tongue, if anything to save myself from a lecture about long-standing family tradition of only granting keys to a student on graduation day. With a short fuse of empathy, I thought, *Oh, my dad the resurrected hardcore conservative.*

Puzzled, I glanced at my phone, "Yeah, my ride's not answering."

"Gavin, it is yes, my ride's not answering. Do you need a lift?"

"Guess so."

"We should get going then."

I reached school on time, but for whatever reason the entire morning felt rushed. The half-mile hike from homeroom to Ms. Broom's classroom made it worse. When homeroom concluded, every morning there was always a traffic jam in the exact center of the school where a wave of boys meet up with a wave of girls scrambling to retrieve books from lockers and get to class.

Since my early morning ritual of loitering in the parking area was no longer part of my day, I never had a chance to catch up with anyone until usually around lunchtime.

Because of the traffic jam, it never failed that I made it to contemporary sociology just as the tardy chime sounded out. Thankfully, Ms. Broom had an open mind about the school's gender segregation policy and understood the delays.

"Everyone in their seats?"

I desperately wanted to question Marissa as to the whereabouts of Jacob, but there were too many eyes around. Mainly Taylor.

As soon as class was over, I met Marissa outside in the hall.

"Where is Jacob?"

"I haven't seen him today, I don't know. Have you tried to call him?" Marissa replied.

"Can't get him. No answer, not even a text."

"Maybe he stayed out too late and drank too much coffee?" Marissa suggested.

Rounding the corner of the main hall, Marissa and I observed some unusual commotion at the other end of the breezeway near the Student Services office. Two officers had someone cuffed whose head was lowered as the police guided them toward the front door. Nearby the uproar, Jayden headed in our direction as the detainee shouted while struggling with the officer. The voice was slurring, almost muffled or from the tone of it, they were clenching their jaw shut.

"Turns out your boy isn't so tough!" Austin growled to Jayden.

As soon as the officers cleared the exit doors, Jayden quickened his step in our direction.

Out of breath, Jayden shared, "Gavin it's Jacob."

"Jacob got arrested?"

That of course was the first thing that came to mind since I'd just witnessed someone being hauled out the front of the building.

"No Gavin, something bad happened."

"What do you mean something bad? Like what?"

"I don't know exactly, just that he was attacked last night. He is in the hospital."

Time stopped. My breathing stopped. My muscles tightened, and I lost the grip on my books and they crashed to the floor as adrenaline took charge, surging through my veins, taking over my body and I bolted for the front door.

Taylor exited one of the bathrooms as I was running and I almost knocked her down. Jayden paced in behind me trying to keep up with my uncontrollable mad dash to the end zone.

Across the courtyard, Jayden and I darted around other students as we sprinted our way to his car. Not sure what, but I was saying something in the rush as we jumped in his car and sped out of the parking lot. Time had stopped, but the action continued. When Jayden's car cleared the courtyard, I caught a glimpse of Marissa and Taylor standing on the sidewalk trying to flag us down. I cursed at

Jayden and warned that he dare not stop. He didn't. Probably nothing short of death could've stopped me from getting to the hospital.

As Jayden conveyed to me what he knew, time remained outside of my grasp for the next half-hour. Nothing mattered, my heart racing, eyes flooding, and all I wanted to do was save Jacob. If dying meant that the night before would have never happened, like before, I could've died right then.

...found common ground.

Jayden's vehicle disappeared from the school grounds.

Taylor faced Marissa, "You have a car right?"

Marissa and Taylor broke from the courtyard and dashed to the parking lot. Not too long after, Chloe and Grace made it out in front of the school near the brick columns.

Inside her car, Marissa struggled with a set of keys, fumbling as she attempted placing the correct one in the ignition. When the car buzzed to life, music loudly blasted out causing Marissa and Taylor to respond with a quick twitch. Marissa reached and turned it off. Soon, they were flying.

Halted by a red traffic signal, Taylor became uneasy looking through the front window where the glass remained stained with the letters BL and OW written in bright red lipstick. Marissa had only erased the center. Taylor developed an urge to say something.

"Eating disorder."

Marissa flicked up a shirtsleeve, "Cutter."

Within seconds, the light signaled green and Marissa, and Taylor reached for the radio at the same time, hoping to relieve an awkward moment.

#

Feverishly, I insisted on calling Jacob's cell phone repeatedly. I'd hoped he might answer and tell me this was all a big misunderstanding and he was fine.

Completely out of my mind, I tabulated the number of rings before my calls redirected to a voicemail recording. Jacob's voice, a happy greeting, only ramped up my emotional turmoil. Not expecting anything, on the fifteenth attempt, someone answered. His voice cracking and somber, Jacob's father greeted the call.

Discombobulated details led me to understand that underneath the tire of a car parked at the crime scene, Jacob's cell phone was discovered. The cops returned the phone to Jacob's father earlier that morning while he and Jacob's mother were at police headquarters for a debriefing. They had found a wallet on the pavement as well.

Once maneuvering through a multi-level concrete deck of parked cars, past a pleasantly welcoming reception area, and reaching a corridor of elevators, the hospital became cold and antiseptic.

The pale colored floors scuffed with black heel marks atop layers of floor-wax held an unsympathetic shine. That floor was the only thing I saw with my head facing downward, and my hearing was limited to the mental looping of Jacob's verve from his voicemail greeting. Though it was a memory in my mind, his voice sounded ever so realistic.

Breaking up the repetitious reverb of a familiar voice were the systematic beeps of various monitors as Jacob's parents guided us through a series of drab curtains.

Passing the last curtain, my hands quivered and my body moved forward though it seemed as if the "me" on the inside wasn't me, but only an observer. My moves were robotic, blending with the machinery buzzing all around.

Though he didn't look it, Jacob was alive in a technical sense. His eyes were swollen shut, there were bruises, his skin torn and stitched and when I noticed the dried blood trapped in his eyebrows, I fell apart. I felt my body limber up and gravitate downward and the inside "me" escaped to places unknown.

I suddenly became a patient and awoke sitting in a chair with a nurse hovering at my side. Shame surged through me, but at least I was close enough to reach out to my side with one hand and touch Jacob, my best friend.

#

In a waiting area, Jacob's parents explained in detail what transpired in that dark parking lot. Marissa, misty-eyed, backed away from the conversation.

Mumbling she said, "I can't handle this." She proceeded toward the nearest restroom. Taylor followed behind and when she entered the bathroom, Marissa was in a stall hidden away.

"What are you doing?"

Quieted by the metal partitions, Marissa answered, "Using the bathroom."

Taylor seemed concerned, "Are you sure?"

"I'm okay."

#

Allowed to visit if only for my sake, Jayden kept his hands resting on my shoulders. When I removed my hands from my face, I had nothing to express but the singular thought that was traveling the playground of my mind.

"He is going make it, isn't he?"

Jayden, in a manly way, tightened his grasp on my shoulders, yet he didn't say anything. I gave him credit for the bravery to stand there.

#

Chloe and Grace were left to head up their senior social status in the cafeteria, alone.

Pecking at a cheese topper Chloe expressed her thoughts clearly, "Weird day."

"Right."

"Grace, do you think Austin really did it?"

"Why would they arrest him if they didn't have proof?"

"When did Gavin and Jacob start being friends again?" Chloe pecked at the food on the tray.

"It surprised me too. I guess that explains why Gavin turned into a goblin."

"Yeah, but why wasn't Jacob in his Halloween costume? I'm so confused."

"Like I said, weird day."

"Yeah, you did say that."

#

Marissa and Taylor were both crying as they headed back to campus.

Taylor mopped mascara from her face, "I'm a complete loser."

"Why is that?" Marissa sniffed.

"Guilt. I was supposed to be there last night and I feel like a complete turd because I ignored Jacob for two years because of something stupid and now…"

"It wasn't your fault."

Angrily, Taylor added, "I knew that Austin was a creep. The only reason I could stand him was because of Gavin. I think Gavin liked anybody who fit into the mold."

Adding up the details, Austin's attack in the forefront, Marissa recalled what she overheard in the media center. She was not able to resist speculating as she fit the pieces together. Back at camp, Gavin hadn't expended too much time talking about Taylor, nothing other than declaring her a snob and someone he'd been friends with forever. When Jacob and Gavin offered Marissa the run down about their school, the specifics with regard to their past and their personal relationships were less important than mapping out plans to stir up the social order.

"Did you and Gavin date?" Marissa questioned curiously.

"I wouldn't call it that. More like close friends. I mean we went on a couple of dates like a couple. It didn't work."

"What about Jacob? Does or did he date?"

Taylor continued wiping her face, "I saw the two of you together and I assumed the two of you were dating."

"Well, yes. Well, I'm not so sure now."

"I thought he was warming up to the idea of dating me."

Marissa winced, "Not so sure about that either."

Taylor snarled, "Why, cause he is only into the vampire thing?"

After a brief pause Marissa answered, "No. I think he might be into the boy thing."

Shocked, Taylor turned to face Marissa, "No way!"

"Not sure, but I overheard something between Austin and that guy back at the hospital, what was his name?"

"Jayden."

"Yes. Sorry I forgot his name."

"Jayden wasn't involved in this was he?"

"No."

"What did they say?"

"Well, Austin saw something sketchy between Jacob and Gavin."

Confused, Taylor said, "Like what?"

"All I heard was," Marissa hesitated, "It was a long hug."

"OMG. Austin has a crush on me. I thought after he saw me and Jacob talking he was pissed off and went and beat the crap out of him."

"Gavin and Jacob were friends before, right?"

Taylor was puzzled, "I didn't know they were friends

now, but yeah," Taylor stopped, thought then suddenly exclaimed, "They – were – really – tight. OMG."

"It's not an issue for me, but OMG is right."

In denial, Taylor added, "Wait, wait, wait. Jacob called twice and invited me for coffee and Gavin and I…I'm so confused right now."

Raising her brow Marissa concluded, "Well, about that…"

#

Sobbing well into the afternoon, I hadn't even considered lunch, by now my hands were shaking, and I required coffee and food. Earlier, one of the friendly nurses tried to get me to at least snack on a Jell-o cup, which I politely declined. It might've been that I didn't respond at all, still floating in and out of my body, I was not sure of either.

If the choice were given, I would've stayed through the night, though I was informed by Jacob's parents that my dad would be there to collect me soon. Only family members were given permission to stay and though we could lie, most likely getting away with it, I knew the idea would never fly with my dad.

Odds are he was going to kill me anyway because my phone battery ran out of charge hours ago. I owed Jacob's parents for the thoughtful communication back and forth with Dad as to my whereabouts and state of mind. Not showing up at home on time after school was a guaranteed three to five months without an allowance, monitored free time and necessitated an open bedroom door policy. That along with the fact that I'd skipped out of the school without letting anyone know.

I covered every side of the hospital bed during my visit. Watching Jacob's ribcage rise and fall occupied my mind and, a couple of times, I inched close enough to his bruised eyes I saw the movement of his eyeballs, all the while praying they would open. As I examined each wound, I began to feel vague pain as if the injuries were my own.

With my hand resting on Jacob's arm, I reflected. "Remember that time we set up that tent in the backyard," I choked, "to make your parents think we were out there sleeping and then we walked around your neighborhood spying on people?" I broke off, sniffing and then pressed my face atop my hand that rested, "Man, just wake up. I'm so sorry for being such a... If I could take it back."

Interesting how trauma could take one down a long winding road called memory lane. Those memories flooded my mind as tears flooded my eyes.

By the time Jacob and I were ten, our status was best friends. Even our parents had become familiar with each other since he and I and our goings-on revolved around the other. There aren't many activities that I remember from my early life that didn't involve Jacob. When I visited my grandparents, Jacob came along. When he visited his, I did the same. Lack of resemblance, genes and blood type affirmed that we weren't twins though our behaviors seemed enough for argument in the evaluation of such, to some degree anyway.

The last time the two of us were in a hospital setting at the same time happened when we were twelve. Bravery got us into a situation in a skateboard park. When I tried to ride a rail for the first time, it didn't work out very well. All I recall was flying into the air full speed and when I came to my senses, I felt a needle plunge into my stinging elbow. The surgeon sewing me together like a ripped pair of trousers hurt worse than the shot of painkiller or the injury itself, for that matter.

Ending our skater phase left me with a bad scar and Jacob with a crooked finger where he'd broken it trying to achieve the perfect landing.

Leaning in I whispered, "Jacob, please wake up."

#

The restricted, cramped room held three chairs, one of which was stationary while the other two were fitted with rotating wheels for mobility. Affixed atop a rectangular table sat a 17-inch monitor, the screen divided into four cubes. Wearing an orange jumpsuit, cuffs locked to a chair, Austin sat leaning forward with his face fixed on the screen in front of him.

On the recording, a brutal beating was underway. Austin recognized his own baseball cap. That blood-splattered hat was long gone, in a heap of trash rolling on a conveyor belt heading for an incinerator. Jacob's face was obvious as the victim, but the camera angle revealed a vague shot of the aggressor. Circumstantial evidence as proof of the crime, Austin had reported his wallet as stolen or lost conveniently just hours following the incident and unknown to him, it lay feet away from Jacob's frail torso.

Since Austin fled in the opposite direction of the single witness, she didn't see his face and only remembered his approximate height, approximate weight, a hat and the dark colored clothing he wore.

Joining Austin, two suited men stood at the corners of the space observing as he reviewed a playback from a security camera recording. Expression dull, never changing, Austin had one response to the recording after smugly reclining back in a chair.

"He's a faggot."

#

135

My strength still eluded me when Dad retrieved me from the hospital. He was barely able to pry me away from Jacob's side and get me to and inside the car. Manipulating my breathing, worry controlled me, and the contemplation ruling the chaos was the notion that Jacob might die before I ever heard him speak again.

In the car, I pressed my face against the side window. The window was cool, but as each street light passed my eyes, I sensed its warmth.

When we turned right onto Haywood Street and I witnessed the do not cross warning on the police tape, my lip twitched, my face flushed with a burning as tears blurred my vision.

Had I stayed at the coffee shop for another half-hour and ridden home with Jacob, would that have changed the outcome? It was another question I would never be able to answer.

I didn't sleep that night.

#

By the time I dragged myself out of bed the next morning Jacob's father had phoned letting Dad know that Jacob's condition was much better than the previous day.

Regretfully, I began screaming at Dad and accusing him of lying to me so I wouldn't put up a fuss about going to school. I calmed down after having coffee and speaking to Jacob's father on the phone for myself.

When I opened my locker, I fought back another round of tears when I saw Caleb's face staring back at me from the rear wall. We all had one, Jacob, Marissa and I.

I appeared quite scary, almost crazy from lack of sleep and stress, and for once, I appreciated Marissa's presence and the tone of her voice.

"Rough night?"

"I didn't sleep. At all."

Looking over my shoulder, Marissa's eyes widened swiftly just as someone shouted my name from behind.

"Gavin!"

Recognizing the voice, I pivoted around and a hand caught my face, casting a crisp smack that echoed in the hall.

In a rage Taylor screamed, "Liar! Two faced liar!"

Holding my stinging cheek, baffled I probed, "What did I lie about?"

Without giving Taylor a second to respond I continued with my next thought, "What did you do to yourself?"

Taylor was different, it was more than just the anger, she was completely baldheaded.

Taylor, in a rage quickly drew nearer, slapping, clawing, and screaming. Chloe and Grace rushed to our sides and latched onto Taylor, pulling her away as she continued kicking and shouting.

"Everybody has gone nuts around here!" I suggested, still rubbing my jaw.

I had no idea why Marissa said, "Our plan is in the can."

Frustration engulfed my reaction, "My God! Are you still thinking about that crap?"

"I…"

Not letting Marissa speak, I interrupted, "I'm sorry. I can't think or talk right now. Somebody tried to kill Jacob and now Buffy the Vampire Slayer is trying to kill me!"

Reminiscent of a morning in a chocolate-brown building, I left Marissa standing alone.

#

Since no one could peel Gavin away from Jacob's bedside on the day he was alerted that Jacob was hurt;

Marissa and Taylor didn't get an opportunity to visit with Jacob. Making the way back to school, Marissa continued telling Taylor about the summer, Gavin's and Jacob's reunification, and their extensive plan for an experiment in human behavior.

That night with Grace and Chloe at her side, Taylor slid a buzzing clipper through her blond locks and the strands fell to the floor. She chose a drab look and though she didn't state specifics of what she discovered, she expressed to the Chloe and Grace that if Gavin and the others wanted spooky she would give them spooky.

Though outraged, Taylor found her own freedom from the chains that had bound her for a long time too. She felt betrayed and used.

Years of following Gavin around mimicking his behavior, willingly going along with every trendy whim and giving him devout devotion as the leader suddenly summed up to be a waste of time and deception.

Taylor's long held fantasy crumbled under the weight of an innuendo. Though her assumptions were not exactly accurate, it was clear to her why certain problems existed between her and Gavin. A long held secret.

Chloe and Grace tried to sway Taylor from doing something so extreme. They were willing to play along with dress up, but actions this exaggerated were a bit much. Jokingly, Grace suggested that Taylor was taking the "Party Monster" theme way too far.

Leading up to Jacob's attack as Taylor, Chloe, and Grace played along with a plan they didn't know existed, Taylor muscled through the backlash with her country club parents.

More than ever, her parents were convinced that she was doping. Never would they understand the truth about what was going on, even if Taylor had had the inside scoop of what Jacob wanted to achieve within the social order. Her parents didn't like games. Study and behave properly. Don't ever scar the family name.

Eventually, the ordered therapy would help Taylor for reasons other than what her parents expected. The revelations in Marissa's car along with the mandated doctor's sessions pushed Taylor to a breaking point.

#

Marissa stalled as Gavin disappeared down one end of the hallway. Chloe and Grace released Taylor in the middle of the other end of the corridor. When Taylor scurried to the restroom, Marissa proceeded in that direction as well.

"Whatever you're doing in there, stop it!" Marissa demanded.

Exiting the stall Taylor responded, "Haven't had lunch yet."

Marissa rested the weight of her body against the counter, "Wasn't that out of hand?"

"Maybe, but don't I have a right to be mad? How do I look? Does this make the three of you happy? Thought I'd introduce something new, plain, bland, and non-descript. You three played me!" Taylor glared at Marissa's reflection in the mirror.

"Our intentions were not to play anyone."

Taylor smoothed her hand across her bald head, "Tell me then."

Marissa rubbed her eyes, "So much has happened. Now it is all so confusing, whatever we were trying to prove."

Taylor smiled, "So now that is two things we have in common."

In that moment, two young women found common ground.

...emotion filled the room.

Giving in to Jayden's persuasion, I agreed to attend afternoon practice. Even though I was thoroughly tired, I needed to tackle something due to the pent up stress from arguing with my dad about going to school and the earlier assault from a reinvented Taylor.

We ran play after play and the constant whistle blowing was beginning to work whatever nerves I had remaining. My teammates got in position and I bent at the waste, peering through the protective grates of the helmet. Perhaps from the tiredness my vision randomly blurred. We completed the play and a whistle sounded.

Lining up again, we positioned ourselves. In front of my hazed vision, when it focused, Austin's face vividly glared straight at me, and I heard his tainted voice.

"I know about you sunshine!"

I lifted to a full stance, violently jerking off the protective headgear. Jayden was hunched to my left and I noticed him step forward looking in my direction.

"Gavin, what's up?"

I slid my fingers through what hair I had left and the sweat covered my hand.

Jayden shuffled closer as my teammates relaxed their stance when a whistle blew.

"Gavin?"

Slowly, I started pacing backward, one foot after the other, until I shifted and trotted across the length of the field.

Jayden shouted out, "Gavin! Gavin!"

The coach blew a series of warning whistles, but I continued picking up speed until I ran at a steady pace. Spontaneously, I hurled my helmet across the field and it hit the turf with a thud. In what seemed a very natural motion, I spit out my mouthpiece, and drool streamed from the corners of my mouth as I raised my arms over my head shaking my fists like I was declaring victory.

Stench from stale clothing and sweaty teen boys hit me the second I shoved the locker room door open. I peeled off the sweaty uniform and flung each article in different directions of the smelly room. Quickly, my hands shoved my underwear past my knees and I stepped my feet out.

In less than four minutes, I had stripped and showered. Standing there, as I came into the world, naked, I finally sensed what had been missing, a complete rebirth.

Dressing, I observed my well-toned body. The dusting of dirty-blond hair on my legs, my calf muscles strong and detailed. My stomach, firm, with each abdominal distinctive and a thin, barely visible line of delicate hair trailed from my navel to my waistline. My pectorals firm, nipples flat, red with limited blond hair.

Slipping into my street clothing, I reflected about Caleb, what he saw; what he would never be. I pondered, though I'm fit, as is Jacob, how undeniably vulnerable the human body is despite the natural capacity to heal. There are limits to the body's remarkable abilities. Limits for someone who is sick, limits for someone who is well and limits for someone under physical assault, in vehicle crashes or otherwise.

On my way out of the locker room, I saw his locker, I balled my fist and punched and cracked the nameplate labeled Austin. Pieces of the lettering tumbled to the stained tiled flooring.

While I weaved through the mismatched buildings, I phoned Marissa and asked her to meet me in front of the school. As I waited, in the distance, I heard the grunts, flesh crashing, and the whistles blowing warnings.

While in her car, most likely I had Marissa terrified. My time bomb was still ticking in conjunction with the movements of a clock on the wall. A couple of times, as I expressed myself, I pounded on the dashboard and went as far as to hit myself while verbally spewing nothing but irrational statements.

"What was I thinking? I-hate-football! Always hated football. His face, his effing face, right in front of me. I'm-so-stupid! Stupid af! That is true hate. Not a front. I get it. I so get it! And that poor kid! All he wanted was to grow up and he had no idea what a complete tool I really am! Now, Jacob's is… uggh and I don't even understand why Austin beat the shit out of him. I mean, it's not like Jacob just started being a dark water swimmer this year!"

As I'd finished ranting, we arrived at the hospital and steered into the parking deck. Marissa didn't comment at all. Maybe she was too afraid to speak. I couldn't blame her.

"Thank you. Catch you later." I walked away from the car.

Seeing Jacob calmed me.

"How are you doing buddy?"

I remained quiet, giving space, wishing he would respond. Shortly thereafter, I rambled.

"Man, things are so out of control. Taylor attacked me today for some reason. Hey, I'm sure you don't know, but they arrested that son of bitch for doing this to you."

I gave Jacob time to say something, anything.

"Oh, get this, I quit football!" I mentioned, expecting some shared enthusiasm.

For a long period, I spoke to Jacob like he might hear every expression and for periods of the visit I sat quietly praying for my friend. Praying for myself. Praying for anyone who'd ever been in my presence. I prayed especially for the fact, that if at any time, my presence had ever caused another human being any unease.

#

Before driving away from the hospital grounds, Marissa phoned Taylor, expressing her concerns about Gavin's erratic behavior. Even though, fuming with feelings of betrayal, Taylor agreed to accompany Marissa back the hospital. During the ride, Marissa explained, "He was pounding on the dash, crazy."

"Maybe he realizes his jig is up."

"Taylor, he seemed oblivious to any of that. I haven't mentioned anything to him about what I heard. How would he know unless you said something? Anyway, it is probably better that you talk to him, under the circumstances. After this summer, I don't think he and I have a safe record for dealing with serious stuff. Besides, you have known him longer. I don't know what to say."

"Do I? The real him? Who is the real Gavin Bailey? The Gavin I know, charismatic clean cut and cocky or Gavin the boy hiding in the closet playing doctor with his longtime companion Jacob."

Marissa rolled her eyes, "That's only an aspect. I'm worried about him. Whichever, this is heavy stuff to deal with in a narrow-minded hate filled world."

#

I scooted a nearby chair closer to Jacob's side. I had a crazy notion that if I got closer, I could hear him answer me; wishfully I prayed.

"She called my name, I turned around, didn't even have time to think. I didn't recognize her. I mean, can you imagine? Taylor. No hair? Wild."

I heard a door open and then within seconds a curtain moved. Marissa and Taylor eased to the foot of the bed.

I said both serious and sarcastic, "You're not going to jump me again are you?"

Controlled, Taylor replied, "Not now. Maybe later."

"Can't wait."

Taylor semi-laughed. Marissa rested herself on the foot of the bed.

"Gavin, I had to come back, I was worried about you."

"Thanks for that, but I'm okay. I've needed to do that for a long time."

Taylor switched to the right side of Jacob.

"He looks so bad," Taylor hesitated before meaningfully saying, "Gavin, I'm sorry."

"Taylor, can I ask what brought that on?"

"We…"

Marissa stood up and faced Taylor, "Taylor don't."

Taylor held up a hand, "It's okay Marissa."

Confused, I questioned, "What?"

Taylor veered her face away from the bed, from me.

"Taylor?" Marissa begged.

Taking a deep breath, Taylor turned around, "No."

Feeling a little freaked out I stood up. Mainly because these two were together, I didn't even know they had met.

"First, what are the two you doing together? Second, the two of you are buggin'. Share with the rest of the class?"

Again, Marissa pleaded, "Taylor this is not the place."

"No! Spill it!" I demanded.

Looking straight at me Taylor confessed, "You? Jacob?"

"Me and Jacob what?"

Suddenly Marissa regretted sharing, "Gavin, I'm sorry.

I told her about something I overheard."

"Okay, this is getting sketchier every second. Overheard what?"

Eyes blazing at me Taylor let it out, "One night after practice Austin saw you and Jacob hugging in the parking lot."

Was this a joke? I wondered. *What are they talking about?*

"Saw us hugging in the parking lot?"

Taylor crossed her arms, "That's what he said."

Searching around in my already chaotic mind, I recounted the recent times that Jacob and I were together in the lot after practice. Oh yeah, after practice, I suddenly recalled.

"Hugging? Jacob was cracking my back; hurt it during practice."

Taylor moved back to the end of the bed, "Gavin, he said it was a long, long hug?"

It took me a second to do the math. It hit me. I sat down.

"Ah. I get it."

I covered my face and a voice clearly rang out in my head.

"I know about you sunshine. I know about you sunshine. I know about you sunshine."

For a show of support, I assumed, Marissa came over and placed her arm across my shoulders.

Taylor proceeded, "Do you want to fess up?"

Taylor was both empathetic and wounded as she reached for resolution and closure.

Uncovering my face, tears welled in my eyes and my lip trembled as it became clearer as to why Jacob had been beaten up. My emotion filled the room.

"I…" I wasn't able to get the words to come out.

Taylor pushed, "Well?"

A struggled whisper rose from the bed, "Don't-answer-that."

Jumping to my feet I demanded, "Get the nurse!"

…nothing wrong with love.

Watching Jacob recover left me with such gratitude that couldn't be expressed with words — nothing that suited how deeply my emotions ran anyway. I found it hard to decline feeling responsible. Maybe if I'd been beaten-up too for the crime that someone deemed needing a sentence these emotions wouldn't exist.

The process was slow, but every day Jacob's strength increased by measurable amounts, and he managed to remain awake for longer periods during the day. When he used his voice for the first time, his request was clear. He demanded that I not answer a certain question. When he finally opened his eyes, he repeated himself even after Taylor and Marissa had left the room.

"Don't you dare answer that question." Spoken with a struggled whisper then his eyes closed and he faded away.

#

Since the first day at Lift Me up, the first day of school, and the first day following a brutal assault, things had changed.

Familiarity set in with witnessing a hairless Taylor, but taking my imagination to the extreme, I never envisioned Taylor and Marissa turning into best friends forever. To the best of my knowledge, Taylor chatted with Grace and Chloe every once in a while, but for the most part Taylor had kicked them to the curb. Perhaps they'd outgrown each other. Perhaps Taylor viewed them as part of the chains that bound her before she freed her mind and her long golden locks.

She finally got over being angry with me, though I suspected that she grasped an inkling of resentment mainly for me keeping my reunion with Jacob a secret. My relationship with her changed in a way, without any other way to explain our friendship other than it was just different from before. We would always share a history together. At least we were real with each other; something we weren't with the crowds we kept guessing.

I found myself passing by the football field a few times a week, only for the familiarity of it, and to wave at Jayden, who I rarely saw anymore. I don't regret my decision about leaving the team, and to keep fit, I took up running which also became a great outlet.

#

I knew something was up by the celebratory tone of Jacob's father's voice when he called telling me that Jacob would meet me in the hospital cafeteria instead of his room. When I arrived, he was proudly hobbling back and forth on crutches like a newborn colt.

Smiling, I praised his effort, "Look at you."

I grabbed us some lunch and we seated ourselves at a table near a window.

"Gavin, I can't wait to get outside."

"You're getting there a lot quicker that I thought you would for sure."

"Since I've been in here I've been intimate with at least ten different people." Jacob kidded.

Several jokes arose from Jacob's observations during his hospital stay. Personally, I thought he would dig the gown since it appeared so unordinary.

"Walking around in this gown is so humiliating. My willy is poking the fabric out in the front so bad it looks like a pup tent."

"Since ten people have seen it, I wouldn't worry about it too much."

"Easy for you to say."

"Dude, the staff has probably seen so many weenies, looking at yours is like looking at a box of crayons."

"Gavin, never compare a man to a crayon. At least up it to a magic marker or something."

"No bonehead. I didn't mean size. I meant quantity and color."

"Anyway. I'm ready to get out of here."

"You had to go and get beaten up and spoil our plan." I joked.

Part of Jacob's lip refrained from moving when he was talking, "The plan got interrupted, but somebody learned something, surely. Well, with the exception of Austin. Even if he knew what was going on, I don't think he would've gotten it."

"I hope they nail his overalls to the wall."

"Not going to happen."

"Sure it is. He almost killed you, Jacob"

"The thing is, see, I'm not pressing charges."

"Shut up! I mean are you kidding me right now?"

"No joke. I couldn't blame anyone who would want to press charges. For me there is something bigger here, so I'm not doing it."

"Jacob, you can't let him get away with this. What kind of message do you think this sends to others? "

"Well, he's not getting off that easy. There are laws. Some things are out of my control. I'd rather Austin get help than do time and come out more jaded than he already is. The next person might not make it."

"It's a hate crime. Well, you're a better person than me I guess."

Jacob turned silly, "Very true."

My mood got serious, "Can I ask you something?"

"Sure."

"When Taylor and Marissa visited, you heard what we were talking about. Why did you say don't answer that?"

"I heard every word. I heard you talking for two days. I couldn't get any words to come out, until then."

"Why did you say it?"

"Of course I didn't know it was him at the time, but when Austin had me pinned, if you could've heard the vile things he was saying to me. Terrible things. Use your imagination. Hate is ugly. Point is, it shouldn't matter. You know who you are and I know who I am."

"Right, you're right. Just all this made up drama that we were this or that and then we stopped being friends because of it, and now we're this and that. Everybody has different scenarios playing out in their heads."

Jacob looked in my eyes, "You and I know the truth. Nothing else matters. Austin didn't see what he thought he saw, but why explain it really? If it was a hug or not a hug, I'm not ashamed."

"You're right."

"Even though there was that time we kissed and stuff, so what? You know just as well as I do there are other guys that can relate. There are girls who are friends that can relate. What's the big deal, really? What, so we're going to hell or something? Going to hell for love? I hold no regrets. We've bonded in many ways. Acts of friendship. Acts of love. I love you. I'm not afraid to own up to it in front of anyone. I'd say it to anyone even if it meant I had to live through someone beating the shit out me."

I reached for Jacob's arm, "I feel the same. You know, Taylor thinks I'm a liar and I'm not in the sense of what she believes is the truth. What she believes happened."

"Like I said, none of that matters. She'll get over it. For the last two years, you two were attached at the hip, I was so jealous. I missed you so badly."

"I love you too, man."

Jacob smirked, "Oh, gosh."

Seriously, I said, "I mean it. And I missed you more than you will ever understand. Every single morning. Every single day."

We would never share our truth with Taylor. Jacob was dead-on when he said that what happened between us had nothing to do with his attack or the reason our friendship fell apart. Of course, it was a small thread of detail in the tapestry of a greater story and we acknowledged that between ourselves.

Whether there was ever a mass confession or not, the percentage of close friends that have shared the same intimacy was bound to be up there, and regardless of society's denial or unwilling acknowledgement, there is nothing wrong with love.

If Austin had never made an assumption about what he thought he saw in the parking lot, no one would've given a second thought to how Jacob and I interacted with each other. Now, that the cards were on the table and due to the tragic circumstances, I understood how the people closest to us could jump to conclusions.

However, with all that happened, I didn't care anymore about what people were thinking or how they felt about us, so I drew closer to Jacob and didn't hesitate showing my feelings, if anything, I did it even more so. Years ago, my attitude about the subject would have been completely different. I had learned that life was fragile, action and consequences can't be taken back.

...made me blush.

Subjects of study in Ms. Broom's sociology class were hitting close to home, and understandably, the subject of hate crimes became our next area of study, while Jacob was held up in a bland room attached to tubes and covered with bandages. The next topic written in stenciled lettering across the expo read, Revolutions that Changed the World. That certainly fit with our mini-revolution underway, geared to reorganize the seating arrangement in the segregated cafeteria.

I was so relieved when I learned that Austin wouldn't be returning to school. I was not sure that I could keep myself from attacking him. It was wrong, but I'm really truthfully honest when I say that I might've hurt him. Time might help me work this out of my system, but forgetting was not an option.

When Austin finished a short stint at a boy farm in Alabama for troubled youth, his parents were sending him to Texas to live with his grandmother where he would be under strict supervision from a stern uncle who operated a cattle ranch. Not only would Austin have to rope cattle, and shovel piles of smelly cow shit, he would have to repeat grade twelve and complete a series of tolerance seminars. A document Austin agreed to and signed specifically stated that if he ever placed his hands on another person in a violent manner while he was a juvenile, there would be no trial and the punishment would be severe.

Jacob's parents shared with us what happened while the District Attorney and lawyers from both sides worked out the complicated punishment that would keep Austin from spending time in a more severe youth detention center.

"He is awake! I didn't kill him." Austin shrugged.

Austin's legal representation tried to get him to realize the extent of what he had done.

"Might be awake, but I don't think you realize how much trouble you're in son. You're free to hate whatever, whoever you want, but physically directing that hate is a whole different ballgame."

Jacob's parents wanted to reach across the cylindrical table and strangle Austin. They didn't agree with Jacob's decision, however, they respected his feelings and wishes. Jacob repeated to them several times that hate is not natural, but a result of being taught, trained and conditioned. Kindly enough, Jacob's heart was open enough to grant Austin a time to heal and hopefully learn that nothing is real; nothing but love. Jacob wished that someday Austin might extend the same respect to someone else.

Though Austin's penalty was more than Jacob wanted, Jacob had no say over the law and the conditions authorities were willing to accept as a compromise.

"You should thank somebody son. This might be the luckiest Friday afternoon of your life. Therapy and community service is a lot better than doing time."

Jacob's parents said Austin didn't say much and given his choices, he signed the agreement as his mother cried and thanked the Lord. Austin's mom thanked Jacob's family later, which I thought was a nice gesture.

I had given my opinion to Jacob and anybody else who would listen. I'd taken into account Jacob's wisdom and what he said was rational and I got it, but trying to wrap it all up with a pretty bow didn't remove my grudge. I still had some growing to do, I guess. The bottoms of my shoes weren't quite as worn as Jacob's, yet.

#

Holidays came and went. I hadn't paid much attention, except for noticing the Christmas trees when I entered the sterile environment of the hospital. Again, one night while I was lounging in my bedroom reading, I heard fireworks booming outside of the window.

When Valentine's Day came around I got a card from Caleb's parents and because of that, Marissa and I drove for a couple of hours and visited with Caleb's family. When the time came for us to leave, Marissa found me sitting on his bed crying. Then we both were crying and Caleb's parents joined in and all but adopted us on the spot. We left our pictures behind in his room and the resemblance Caleb and I shared coiled another level of sentiment.

It is a wonder that I made it through grades ten and eleven without Jacob, because I missed him so badly during the days of year twelve as he recovered. When he returned to school, I eventually settled down and became more alert of life around me.

Jacob missed close to a couple months of classes and, lucky for him, he had a majority of the credits that were required for graduation. As soon as he was able, we started working on class assignments in the hospital lounge, sometimes his room, and that was a lot of fun until we would fall asleep while studying art history. I'd wake up, get home and would have to endure the wrath of my dad for missing curfew. I was happy that the lectures were all I got and not a sentence of house arrest.

Dad had lightened up since my trip to camp, even letting me take his car to visit Jacob. I concluded Dad had obviously observed positive adjustments of my general carriage.

Jacob and I had no idea that my dad had spoken to

Jacob's parents with regard to his concerns about my arrogance. It wasn't by chance that we ended up at "Lift Me Up" together. It was upon the suggestion of Jacob's parents; Dad inquired about the camp and decided that that was exactly what I needed.

I don't remember exactly who said what, but one of Jacob's parents accidentally slipped up and mentioned my dad and the camp; not that it was a big secret kept from us, however. Even so, I still believed in the deck of cards.

#

How could I use the word normal to explain the return to the daily routine with Jacob present, Austin gone, and the changing of friendship status all around? The only possible way was to call it the new normal, because that was exactly how our lives were then.

The new normal and the workings of the universe aligned Jacob, Taylor, Marissa and myself with tuxedos and formal gowns. For several weeks, or so I heard through the high school gossip line, there was much speculation about what Taylor, Marissa, Jacob, and I might pull off for prom night. The stories floating around the school for a little over a month now were endless. Rumors produce funny results, like the day one of my former coaches pulled me aside, asked me if I was using drugs and informed me that within the entire coaching team there was discussion of planning an intervention.

But back to prom. We showed up later of course, but it was not an intentional tardiness. While timing out the evening plans we didn't account for how long it would take to slip a pant leg over Jacob's injured ankle nor how time consuming it was when someone had to struggle with crutches.

The four of us dressed relatively standard for the

occasion with our choice of suits and gowns. There wasn't much that I could do about my hair and Taylor only had stubble growing on top. Taylor insisted on doing Marissa's make up and every time Marissa reached for the eyeliner, Taylor smacked her hand.

Taylor finally calmed down with regard to feeling deceived and lied to. Jacob said she'd get over it and she did eventually. I couldn't pinpoint it, but something had changed in Taylor too. She seemed lighter in an emotional sense and I reckoned it was a side effect caused by the missing weight of her flowing blond locks.

There were times in the weeks that followed the memorable smack in the face that I felt so bad for Grace and Chloe. At the beginning of every school week they'd show up with a new look. I'm not sure if anybody shared with them what was going on behind the scenes. Sure, Taylor had gotten them on board, but if Grace and Chloe had knowledge of what Taylor learned from Marissa about the plan, I didn't know. I never asked.

Several times, I thought about clueing them in, but I decided to let it go. Grace and Chloe were caught in the middle of a set of circumstances that I was sure had them just as confused as the rest of the student body.

As proven once before, we had all taken different directions with our lives in a short period. Like a game of twenty-one, there was a hand of fifteen on the table and the dealer dealt a nine. Jacob and I knew the game all too well.

We had certainly disappointed our fellow prom goers by showing up to the dance bland and boring. So kind, Jayden escorted both Chloe and Grace and the poor guy looked utterly embarrassed. Whatever Chloe and Grace pulled from the brain of James St. James and his outrageous recount of club life in New York City wasn't translating on the canvas of color. There are colors in the spectrum that simply don't go together.

As a group, we slithered our way to the middle of the dance floor because it was the least likely place for someone to bang Jacob's injured foot. It became obvious to me that all eyes were honed in on us since there were as many rumors scampering around the classrooms as there were cockroaches hiding in the center-block walls, and *they* were probably wondering what might happen.

One day during school I'd discovered a small neatly folded sheet of paper in my locker that someone shoved through the vent cracks and when I unfolded it the deliverer had hand penned the message, "you dick sucker". It confirmed my suspicions. I didn't get bent out of shape about it. Ignorance and hate exist, that is a fact I had to face. If we had spread the truth, would anyone have believed it anyway? Not likely. Drama is much more fun in a world filled with theatrics.

I thought the note fit right in with Ms. Broom's topic of hate crimes, so I posted the paper on the board next to subject's title. Ms. Broom didn't find it amusing.

Jacob, Taylor, Marissa and I sort of all danced together, like a couple, yet with four people. In the midst of a slow song, instinctively and without any pondering, I leaned my head forward, Jacob did the same and we pecked an off-center kiss on the lips.

Taylor swayed her head back, "I don't care and I'm not going to ask." Then she smiled.

I laughed, "That was nice. Soft lips."

I noticed the arms nudging the heads up and peering eyes shooting in our direction on the dance floor. Taylor leaned in, Marissa followed suit and those two united in a kiss that made me blush.

"Hot." Jacob blurted loudly.

Next and probably looking very interesting from afar, the four of us met in the center and managed a substantial quadruple kiss. I expected a teacher to snatch us out of there, those conservatives. As we separated, we started laughing and much to my surprise Jayden came over and gave each one of us a hug.

…like Thelma and Louise.

Leaving the school cafeteria for the last time, I witnessed a group of eleventh graders sitting where my group sat the year before.

"Look, look at that guy. Complete scrubber!" One said.

Another exclaimed, "Next year we're seniors and then we'll be out of here."

"I'm stoked about the summer. We need to raise the roof!"

Later, at the passing of the torch ritual, I'd also pass along some advice. They had a lot to learn.

I walked the long route out of the building since it was the last day I would ever see those halls again, halls that held many memories, both good and bad. I entered the ninth grade with the notion that I knew everything. Four years, a stone's skip in time, I realized I knew nothing. My height had increased, my body was less lanky, my arrogance had been put in check, and my journey to becoming a man was underway.

#

I refrained from overdoing it with beer pong and tequila twister, but I'd had just enough to keep my mouth flowing with words of wisdom for the incoming senior class. Time would tell if they had paid attention. The walls of the school would have to bear witness to that story as it unfolded.

Not surprisingly, on graduation day, I had a few battles with the alarm clock and overslept. I might've snoozed right through the ceremony, but I heard a knock, I heard the door creep open and my dad's pleasant familiar way of making a statement.

"Gavin, you are going to be late. This is not an example of responsibility."

I stumbled to the coffee maker and slurped down a few cups. I dressed as fast as I could manage and before I finished getting my shoes on, I heard the original sound of a 1967 Volkswagen Karmann Ghia outside the window. Music was blaring from the car and I was expecting my dad to rush out and warn Jacob about the homeowner's association.

I jumped in the car, "Hey Thelma."

"Hey Louise."

Jacob and I veered into the parking area at exactly the same time as Marissa and Taylor. Jacob had to rush off because he was giving a speech and Marissa, Taylor, and I hurried to find a place to sit.

Jacob spoke eloquently.

"As I stand here we are just a heartbeat away from our next journey. A heartbeat has many rhythms. A beat when we are happy."

In my mind, I pictured Caleb and me roasting marshmallows.

"A beat when we are sad."

I reflected back to Jacob's bruised face.

"A beat when we are stressed or mad."

I reviewed flashes of a bathroom stall and a shard of glass.

"Even hate carries its own tune."

I thought of Jacob's face being pounded into the ground.

"Sometimes a beat can stop."

An image of a white sheet hiding Caleb's lifeless body flooded my mind.

"A new journey is never promised, so it is important to

appreciate the one you are on. Every heartbeat, every heartbeat. Heartbeats, both good and bad. As we slide through life let us remember."

I wasn't the only one crying.

Our last gathering in the school parking lot signaled an end and a beginning. Jayden, Chloe, and Grace passed by telling us to have a good summer and we responded likewise. Taylor ended up running over and giving Chloe and Grace a goodbye hug. There was still hope for their reunification, because they were all attending the same college in the fall. It was bound to happen and they would be shopping at Saks soon enough. After all, Taylor had a hot mess to clean up with those two. Even if she had to train them how to use a thrift store wisely or explain that, their ideas for looks from the "Shockumentary" weren't meant to be taken literally.

Jacob looked so dapper in his crisply starched white shirt and tie.

I stepped closer to him, "There is only one more thing to do to make our last day at high school complete."

Jacob flicked his brown wedge, "What's that?"

I reached out, grabbed hold of his shirt pocket and ripped it off.

Marissa applauded, "Nice!"

Jacob chuckled, "I bet you wanted to do that months ago!"

We begin laughing and Taylor didn't quite get what was so funny, but she did have something to say.

Looking puzzled Taylor said, "You two act like Thelma and Louise."

…epilogue

time passes by…

With one gentle tug, he pulls money from my hand, pivots on the heel of one foot, and casually walks away. I watch as he reaches the other end of the congested school hallway joining a huddled group of friends. In that space with great clarity, I realize that my son is no longer a little boy. He is a teenager.

Perhaps it is the familiar sterilized scent of the building or the undetectable flickers from the intrusive fluorescent lighting or possibly the high-octane puberty all around, but something instantly causes my middle-aged mind to flood with memories of days, that at this point in my life, I can hardly believe ever existed. It is cliché to say it, but it seems just like yesterday that I was the young man who wouldn't dare hug his father in front of peers. The embarrassment wasn't worth it even if he had made a special trip to dish out money for some socially significant school activity.

Observing your own children as a middle-aged man, it is difficult to recall a time when you walked the same halls that your children do and remember that you once wore the same shoes. It is always important to me to keep an open mind and try to understand what my son might be going through in his own life.

It is true that I sometimes discover myself saying words to my children that I swore would never come out of my mouth. It is a fact that my son rolls his eyes and has periods of defiance just as I had as a boy.

It is a stretch for younger people to grasp the idea that their parents survived the same trials and tribulations.

S.L. Mauldin

Generations will come and go, society will evolve, but at the core, the experiences are much the same.

My son dislikes being called J.C. and though he knows how his full name, Jacob Caleb, came about, he will never know or fully understand the amount of love that is held in its meaning.

When J.C. was, eight years old he complained to me that other kids would tease him and say, "J.C. gotta pee". Like my dad, I'd lecture with whatever advice I had to offer about bullying. Meanwhile, I felt bad for him and laughed on the inside. Kids can be cruel. Telling a kid that things get better never feels like enough. I'd find myself overcompensating by making sure he had the right shoes. It's hard to say where J.C. stands in the social order; he has friends, he seems happy and that is more important to me than anything.

Through my college years, I remained in touch with Taylor and we'd hang out during the seasonal breaks. We started another intimate relationship over one of the Christmas holidays. It began with eggnog and ended the next morning when we got dressed. I went to Taylor's wedding a year after we were out of college and once life got in the way, our communication became limited to emails, greeting cards, and sending hellos if we'd happen to run into mutual friends. Since then our visits were left up to high school reunions.

We heard years after high school that Austin had gotten in a bar fight in Texas and served some time. Blowing my mind, Jacob hopped on a plane, flew to Texas, and offered to save Austin's ass again. I found it hard to get my head around it, but Jacob said that Austin was very receptive and from what he found out, Austin was defending himself and wasn't the cause of the bar fight. The statute of limitations of the agreement he signed from his first assault had expired, but the judge decided not to overlook it just to remind Austin about what should never happen again. When the judge issued the short sentence, he suggested to Austin that bars were not a good place to hang out. Sitting in front of a bar could lead to sitting behind bars.

Two years after high school, I found out that Jayden came out to his family while he was home from college. I remembered his brave gesture from that night at prom, what our actions must've meant to him as well as a sign of his approval. Perhaps we gave him the courage to be at ease with what hid in his dark corners, which led to his freedom from the closet prison.

Jacob and Marissa became life-long partners and they followed in Sarah's footsteps trying to save the world. I wasn't surprised at all. I never thought the corporate handcuffs suited either one of them. Marissa made a small fortune from a book she published about the human condition and she frequently wrote articles for papers around the country. Jacob's parents had money and Jacob had a trust fund, so he never needed to work in the first place. They adopted five kids and had plans to adopt more.

Jacob, Marissa, and I remain close. J.C. refers to them as an aunt and uncle and their children his cousins. Their children refer to me as an uncle. For the most part, we act as an extended family.

Marissa wasn't insecure about Jacob and I being close. Only close friends, nothing more, though hugging, lying on the couch together and a kiss on occasion was not out of order. When a situation involves only adults and we've had too much to drink, Marissa asks if she needs to separate the two of us or tells us to take it to a closed room.

When I graduated, I went to work with my dad and began preparing to take over the business since he was ready to retire. I got married a few years later to someone I met in a business meeting. Later, Jacob Caleb was born and tragically, not too long after, his mother, my wife, lost a long battle with breast cancer. Needless to say, it was a very tough moment in our lives.

When J.C. joins his friends and they disappear down the hallway, I feel an urge to catch up with him and give him a hug whether it embarrasses him or not. I don't, but I want to. Something about those fluorescent lights, the high-octane puberty, and the scent of the school left my mind reeling about a time I could hardly believe ever existed.

The End.

Made in the USA
Columbia, SC
08 March 2018